And others, Marquis of Lorne

Three Notable Stories

Love and Peril, to Be, or not to Be the Melancholy Hussar

And others, Marquis of Lorne

Three Notable Stories
Love and Peril, to Be, or not to Be the Melancholy Hussar

ISBN/EAN: 9783337279417

Printed in Europe, USA, Canada, Australia, Japan

Cover: Foto ©Andreas Hilbeck / pixelio.de

More available books at **www.hansebooks.com**

THREE NOTABLE STORIES

LOVE AND PERIL

TO BE, OR NOT TO BE

THE MELANCHOLY HUSSAR

RESPECTIVELY BY

THE MARQUIS OF LORNE, K.G.

MRS. ALEXANDER

THOMAS HARDY

LONDON

SPENCER BLACKETT

35, ST. BRIDE STREET, LUDGATE CIRCUS, E.C.

1890

CONTENTS

LOVE AND PERIL

LOVE AND PERIL

A Story of Life in the Far North West

BY

THE MARQUIS OF LORNE, G.C.M.G.

CHAPTER I.

THERE is an amount of egotistic vanity about us that makes us fond of recalling our exploits and acts, however silly these may have been. I do not believe that anybody looks back with the horror that novelists imagine men must feel, even upon such a deed as the slaying of a man. On base murder they may look back with horror; but even then the revengeful feeling which prompted the attempt lives on in the breast of

B

the slayer, and he is apt to think of his work with some of the gratification of satisfied anger rather than with remorse. So, at least, it has seemed to me, judging from instances that have come under my observation, both among savages and civilised men.

Unless something we have done brings to us misery of some kind, either poverty or danger or difficulty, we do not regret our actions. When we suffer from them, then, indeed, do we say, "Why the deuce was I fool enough to do it?" but in this bad world, bad works are not always followed by suffering, and it becomes a daily wonder to those who believe in the prompt return of a sowing of wickedness in a harvest of destruction, how the cause of wrong is so often apparently triumphant.

But I am moralising too much, and the

observations I have made are only due to this—that I once was held by my friends to have behaved in a very silly manner; and yet I did not at all regret it. On the contrary, I look back with interest, amusement, and even joy to the days when I was acting rather the part of a wild man of the woods than the part taken in real life by your humble servant, John Uptas, Esq., of Toronto, Canada, now barrister-at-law, and doing fairly well in my profession as the times go. I have not yet got a silk gown, but the prospect of such a garment is not far; and Osgoode Hall, the great building where we plead in the Provincial Courts, sees many a more forlorn countenance than mine, and many a figure far more bent, pacing the corridors and passing the handsome Italian doorways of its solid architecture.

Gowns and law used not to be to my taste. I was always of an active spirit; and stories read in boyhood of adventures in the Far West, made me think that the life of a Hudson's Bay trapper gave a career far finer than that of most generals. What was the knocking over a few battalions at a distance with heavy artillery, compared to the glory of taking single-handed the life of a grizzly bear? These impressions continued to exercise their sway on my mind; and I could not stand college. I loved Professor Wilson, and admired the talents of several of the gentlemen who adorn the chairs of the University; but I fled with a friend from their seductions, and resolved, come what might, that a few years among the hunters and trappers should harden my body, and, as I thought also, improve my mind.

Several of us students fell to talking about such aspirations one evening at supper. I felt tolerably independent, having a few dollars invested in good funds, my heritage from a frugal father, and I magnanimously offered to pay the way for the chum I had asked to accompany me. We both resolved to throw learning to the winds, and to start as soon as might be—where, goodness only knew. Not to the United States. We were patriotic, and we knew that our own North land afforded opportunity enough for adventure. Westward, of course — westward the course of the Empire takes its way. We drank a good many times to the success of our journey. But morning brought neither hot coppers nor repentance.

In less than a fortnight's time we had made what little preparations we needed, and we were off by the Grand Trunk Railway to Detroit and Chicago. At that time our own great national enterprise, the Canadian Pacific Railway, was in the air, or at most hidden away in the brains of some enthusiastic gentlemen who were looked upon as having more imagination than ballast in their composition. But Chicago was, of course, already a fact. Thither we proceeded, but stayed only a short while among its straight and multitudinous streets. The weather was fine. It was summer. We passed on to places in the head waters of the Red River of the North, as it was then called, and loving river life, we took to the steamers, and then to boats, and ultimately arrived at Fort Garry, the modern Winnipeg.

From thence I remember writing to our dear Professor Wilson at the University, a letter which was a sort of payment of what the English call "conscience money," when they send to their Finance Minister the arrears on their terrible Income Tax. Thus my letter was a kind of acknowledgment of the debt I owed to our Alma Mater, and the best beloved man there.

I had been struck by the accounts of the great freshets that took place, and still take place, in the Red River during the spring-time. Of old these floods caught very many of the buffalo herds that grazed in the wide and rich pastures on the banks of the great stream. The buffaloes were swept away in hundreds, nay in thousands, and I connected this in my mind with what I had read of the vast amount of mammoth ivory and skeletons of elephants found at the mouths of the giant rivers of Siberia. Was it not possible that the deposits of extinct mammals owed their origin to like causes? May not herds of elephants as numerous as the herds of our "American Bison" have grazed in olden days on the Prairies of Siberia near those rivers, and may not these spring floods have carried hundreds away, and drowned them, and strewed their carcases along their banks, and at their estuaries, just in the same way as the Red River drowned its thousands of buffaloes, and strewed its banks with their bodies?

I thought I should never see Toronto again, and this was my tribute at parting to its learning. We did not pause at Winnipeg except to recruit supplies, but passed on down the stream until the broad expanse of its lake lay before us. Then on its bosom we voyaged many days, until we came to where the gigantic Saskatchewan enters it through a vast region of marsh, and sedge, and grass-grown flats, where my classical studies called up remembrances of Virgil's description of the Danube, to whose banks he was exiled. There he bewailed his fate, and the frozen wilderness, and longed for the fleshpots of Rome. Not so I. We shot bitterns, and ducks, and pelicans, and geese by the score, and I was in Paradise. And then, getting Indians to aid us, we canoed onwards up the immense river, westward, ever westward.

We had no lack of food—our guns gave us all we needed. Oh, the delight after our tame town life to be our own masters, our own purveyors! Oh, the charm of those evening camp fires when we had our meals! We two stretched ourselves before the fire, made up of willow and poplar wood, and smoked our pipes, and dreamed of further adventure and exploration.

Only one thing there was to disgust us. Often, after rain, along the prairie paths by the side of the water we came on extraordinary-looking beasts or large lizards. Hideous, bloated-looking things they were, that lifted their fat tails above their broad backs, and waddled rather than ran on their fat legs before us among the grass. But we had little time for the study of natural history. All that was not eatable was disgusting, all that was eatable we appreciated.

And so we voyaged on until we came to the settlement of the Half Breeds, the Metis, as they call themselves, below the "Forks" — the place where the twin rivers of the North and South Saskatchewan join. Here we were in a wooded fir country, with numerous settlements of these people. But onward still we went, now by land, for the travelling was easier on the wooded banks, the forest being not dense enough to impede advance. So we journeyed to the bastioned stockade of Fort Carlton, where was a strong Hudson Bay post, with stores of skins and food, and hearty welcome. Here we determined to go further north, and we crossed the river to its northern bank.

My companion had up to this time evinced nothing but a desire to accommodate himself to my ideas, a frame of mind highly creditable, as I thought, to him, for was I not the author and originator of this journey? What could any opposition to my views do, but destroy harmony and progress?

But the winter was coming on, and I
detected a certain amount of desire on his
part, to accommodate himself to the wishes
of some of the young clerks at the establishment, who told him he could get plenty
of shooting and fun there without going
further. This was not to my taste, and
at first he took my counsel, and said he
would go on with me. Sometimes, however, he forcibly suggested we should
remain. I as forcibly suggested we should
proceed. I prevailed.

We were to go on upon a well-known
route, which, although it involved hard
travelling, was a beaten path. But he
wanted to keep nearer the river, where
we were told we should meet with more
game, in the shape of geese and ducks,
for a week or two longer. The end was a

compromise, always a stupid thing. So we set out, carrying on a toboggan (for snow enough was now falling to make the dragging of a toboggan possible) all our stores. Then came all our difficulties.

At first we shot game enough. But the marches became very wearisome. We carried snow-shoes, and we used them for the first time. No one who has not had experience of this mode of travelling, can imagine how tedious progression on snow-shoes becomes to one unaccustomed to the exertion. To European ears the word often signifies quick and easy progression. The Norwegian snow-shoe, a long board with a strap for the feet, is the instrument that comes to an old country mind. Our snow-shoes are very different. Imagine a large tennis racquet like a heart, but without the indentation at the broad end, which is shaped into an even curve. There is a space left in the cross catgutting for the toes, over which straps are looped. At first all goes well, and the even tramp, tramp, although monotonous, has the sense of novelty. Then you get into a snowdrift, there may be some small accident—an upset —which only provokes mirth. But after hours and days the ball of the toes is apt to get very sore—the *mal de Racquet*, as the French call it—and then how tiresome becomes the march, and how the feet ache and ache!

The temperature became cold in the evenings, and the nights were far from warm. But we found fuel in the copses that fringed the north bank. I always urged that we should strike north, where the country was more full of firs, but the counter-plea was urged, " Let us stick to the river for a few days yet." My companion suffered more from his feet than I did, and became more and more " cross " every evening when we made camp. I had now to go to cut the firewood, for he was so tired and footsore that he always declared that he could do no work when we came to a halt, but help to cook at the fire.

He thought me unreasonable; I thought him opinionative. The marches were not long enough for me; they were too long for him. Finally, we quarrelled outright. Fatigue had made our tempers short, although the day's work was still long enough. It became colder and colder. We had but one good robe (a buffalo skin) with us, and this had to be shared by us both at night. But soon

my friend became so angered with me—
whether it was because I was always too hope-
ful and cheerful, whatever the circumstances,
or because I had "given it him back" when
he had been too abusive in a gloomy fit, or
whether because he had resolved to go no
further whenever he had a chance of re-
turning, I know not; but he would hardly
speak to me. I showed my dislike of this
conduct, and absolute silence reigned between
us.

But while his head got worse, as I thought,
I observed that his toes got better. He was
able to march fully as well as I, and I sometimes thought that he was trying to punish
me by walking me down. But *my* toes got
better too, and I was determined to walk
him down. So we plodded on, and his
silence and sulkiness remained. It was a

ridiculous position. There we were, two lonely mortals, holding to our course, but getting more uncomfortable and doubtful of our own wisdom evening after evening.

CHAPTER II.

AS the blue shadows on the snow vanished, and gave place to the advancing dusk of night, we searched keenly for willow clumps that could afford shelter and fuel, and having come to some suitable spot we silently halted, turned our toboggan, with its load, on edge, so as to afford shelter for the fire which we soon had alight. Then, taking out our robe, we lay close together, cold in body and in manner, but rolled as near together as possible, for the sake of the animal warmth our bodies afforded to each other.

I had become the more energetic of the two, and one evening as we continued our march I found that my companion and whilom friend was lagging behind. I saw it, I am ashamed to say, with delight. "Now I will make him speak," thought I, with malicious joy. On I went, tramping the snow with even footfall, on and on. At last, after we had passed some likely places for a camp, I heard a voice behind me. Was it indeed my friend, who had found speech at last ? Yea, verily ! "—— it, Uptas, we must stop now. Where do you wish to go ? " Another oath. I felt half tempted to give no reply, but I relented, and said : " All right, old fellow ; we'll stop here."

The ice was broken, and we lay down after a surly conversation had taken place.

My friend declared he would take the first opportunity to go back, and I did not demur to his proposition. But we must first find the regular trail, and some Indian lodge or voyageur's tent. We knew well enough that we could best find such to the north of our present position, and we determined to strike for the chain of posts due north. It was a relief to have thus decided.

We had gone some considerable distance too far to the west, but by making an angle to the N.E. we should strike the regular route to Fort à la Crosse by Pelican Lake. I remember that night as we were about to turn in, and were still discussing our pemmican at the fire, we suddenly saw standing close to us the solitary and silent form of an Indian. How he had got so near us we did not know. There he stood like an apparition, so motionless and statuelike was he. Not a sound had escaped him, not a rustling of his snow-shoes had betrayed him as he approached. Wrapped in a blanket, with a short bow in his hand, he stood and gazed solemnly, mournfully, as it seemed to me, at us. We offered him some food, which he took in his hand without a gesture or word. There might be others near us, and I had not got used to the presence of such mysteriously appearing guests.

But there was no reason for suspecting him of any evil design. He departed soon into the darkness. We agreed to keep watch by turns, but slumber overcame both of us, and we saw and heard no more of our friend. Yet I shall never forget that suddenly appearing figure, rooted apparently to the ground, and gazing down upon us, looking in the firelight like a carven figure, or the genius of those wild, steppelike lands. I knew now that I should soon be alone with such companions, for my friend had made up his mind to abide no longer than he could help in this wilderness.

As I went to sleep, the scenes of my journey arose again before me — the turbid rush of the Red River; the low banks cut in the rich soil; then the endless expanse of Lake Winnipeg; the dreary flats and sedges and rapids at the mouth of the Saskatchewan, the wide estuary of that river gradually narrowing as its sides became higher; the firs on the ridges; the stockades of Carlton Fort with the surrounding hills, often lit up vividly by the orange fires of the Canadian sunsets; the recent weary marches; the cold and yet the beauty of

the snowy landscape; and I longed as I
fell asleep for the murmuring shelter of
the pines, and resolved to hasten our march
to the trail, and the abodes of the gallant
pioneers of the fur trade, whose camps we
must find again as soon as possible.

My newly reconciled friend was still
asleep by my side when I awoke in the
morning, and how the cold struck down
on my head and between my shoulders!
I shivered and jumped up, to stamp about
and get all ready for a start, for now that
we had settled to get quickly to some
place where we might find white men,
despondency seemed left behind like the
cold night. How the sun glistened on the
frosty willow boughs and white carpet of
snow! How crisp and bracing felt the delightful air, making the pulses tingle and

redoubling the strength! We started by compass. It was astonishing how hard the prairie had already become. The lakes that we passed were also frozen.

Desiring some change in our diet, for the geese and ducks had now all gone to the south, and we had found none for some time, we resolved to try our lines at a lake. The pemmican was very "stodgy," and we were soon tired of it, although it was well made. Often there is nothing in it but dried meat pounded up, and then poured with a lot of melted fat into a bag. But ours had been carefully made with good berries, so that it was not disagreeable. Still, a few fish would be a pleasant variety. But now we found to our dismay that the lake was so alkaline that there were no fish in it. This was another argument in favour of getting altogether away from the flatter country of the alluvial earth, which is furrowed so deep by the Saskatchewan stream. We resolved on two or three forced marches, and were glad to find again the land swelling into hillocks crowned with fir-trees. Among these there were again pieces of frozen water, and near the first we camped after some days of toil, resolved, if there were fish, to rest a little.

What joy to find a "nibble" at the end of the line, let down through a hole made in the ice! The water was large, the further shore being all fringed with pine. We might hope for good fishing. What was this, the first catch? It was a good one, for the tugs at the line were furious. But there was a slackening of the efforts of the fish, and cautiously I hauled him up to the ice. Another tug, a sudden cessation of all feeling of weight. Good heavens, have I lost him? No; there he was at it once more; but I pulled him steadily through the ice, and lo, a splendid trout lay gasping on the skyward side. Well done, pemmican bait! But perhaps a piece of this fish would serve for another. Let us try. Some time elapsed before there was any reply vouchsafed to the temptation let down into the waters. Then came a jerk, then a long, strong pull. We had another! A similar fight with this, not so prolonged, took place, and there soon lay beside his mutilated comrade another fish, but not this time a trout. It was a " whitefish" or " coregonus," a kind of grayling, much liked by all the dwellers within reach of the lakes, great or small, in North America, for of this fish men never tire. Of trout one can soon have too much. This is not so with the whitefish, so we were rejoiced at getting one.

We were more determined than ever to make a stay at a place where we could have rest and good refreshment. Some more fish were caught, and we went to camp, lighting a large fire near a little frozen stream. The fish were placed on the surface of a little pool close to the fire, and there we left them, content to stretch ourselves near the flames and smoke our pipes, and look upward into the dark boughs that seemed to breathe comfort and warmth after the snow glare of the open plains. Some of the fish were split and put before the fire on sticks, and very good they were.

But what was our astonishment, some time after supper and pipes had been discussed, to find that in a little surface pool formed by the melting of the brook ice by the heat of our fire, several of the fish, captured hours before and frozen stiff, had become alive, and were deluding themselves into the belief that they were about again to become free trout and whitefish. We undeceived them; but that they could come alive again after so prolonged an apparent death was startling and new to us. Whenever we caught them afterwards we did away with the hope of this resurrection by knocking them on the head. So passed this evening, and a good many more, for we were loth to leave our quarters.

The winter became more intense in cold, but that we looked for, and we were astonished at the comparatively small amount of snow that fell, as compared to what we had been accustomed to in Ontario. We certainly never felt so well in Toronto as we did here, on the border of what the geographers rather affectedly call the Sub-Arctic Forest.

We had made several excursions to look for deer, whose tracks we had observed on the border of the lake, and one day I came upon a fine buck, who appeared to be seeking some open water near its shore. He stood still, apparently listening to some noise I must have made, his dusky brown form clearly defined against the snow. My rifle laid him low, and we held high carnival over his flesh, which was excellent. It was a reindeer or Cariboo.

About two weeks later we moved on,

and the ice being firmer with the increased cold, we had no difficulty in crossing several lakes whose waters stretched in the direction we wished to take. It was at the end of one of these marches that we saw smoke from fires kindled on the bank beneath the clumps of firs and willow. One of the pleasures of travelling in the wild parts of the Canadian North-West consists in this, that although in the United States you may be uncertain what welcome may await you among the Indians, in the British territories there is no fear to be apprehended from them. Some events I shall have hereafter to mention, which may seem to prove the contrary, came from accidental and purely temporary causes, the Redskins having been led away by their kinsmen, the Half Breeds.

We therefore approached the encampment without any apprehension, and went in among the lodges of the Indians as though we had been long expected. And their manner to us was quite the manner you would regard as usual among your own relatives, who may have been accustomed to see you go out and in among them. The elders said absolutely nothing. The younger members of the party came forth from their shelters to look at us, and that was all. We sought the Chief's lodge, and found him before his wigwam. He listened as we asked him if all was well, and if we could stay with him. "Tukayow, it is cold," he said; "how many are you?" "Nesho," we replied, "Two only," and we held up two fingers to emphasize our assertion. "Nipakak," he said, after a pause, for the night had fallen, and this meant that we were to sleep; so we made our camp near to the Indians, and soon obeyed the Chief, for our slumbers were very sound.

Next day, my companion forthwith made inquiries as to the means of getting back to Carlton, and on his promising a reward,. an Indian undertook to guide him there, so that he should arrive in a few days' time. I told them I would stay with them, and the announcement was received with a grunt, apparently of satisfaction. We parted rather sorrowfully, although we had fallen out by the way.

Now comes the beginning of my serious adventures. All adventures in love are serious, although they may seem to be of no importance at the time. Yet they leave traces in a man's future, and the evidences of the attachments of other days creep up when least expected. So I ought to have thought, but I did not, and when I found that this old Chief had a daughter who was certainly. pretty, "as Indian ladies go," I am afraid that I was guilty of directing too many of my looks and too many of my remarks in her direction. She was the only daughter of "Okimow," or the Chief, and although I never think that the Red damsels can compare for one moment with the beauties of Toronto, I have to confess that by the side of her native lakes and under the shades of her native pines she was indeed beautiful. She had some fanciful long-winded name, comprising at least two sentences of meaning, something to the effect of "She is the one to whom all listen when she talks," but I could not get my tongue round so much of this lingo, and I called her "Kiooshka," which was some imitation of her father's word for "daughter." She managed my name very well when I once graciously took pains to teach it to her. She often came after us on short expeditions, asking to carry something, and I began to fear with a sort of sweet misgiving that I had made too great an impression upon her. Why should she always wish to carry things for me, to look after my camp, to let me find a charming pine-twig bed always ready for me when I came back from hunting deer?

I had misgivings, but I manfully suppressed my misgivings, as most men do under the circumstances, and I allowed things to happen which in civilised society might have been held as "compromising." But how could I help it? This dear little maiden, with her quick brown eyes, and cheeks of deep nut-brown, with the glow of healthy blood making them flush a lovely dusky red, was my camp-maker, and guardian spirit in my loneliness. I could only get grunts from most of her kindred. She had always a smile for me, and never for an instant allowed anything to mar my comfort as far as lay in her power. This is a trait in woman which is universally appreciated.

"DEAR me, what an angel Kiooshka is!" I used to say to myself, as I stretched myself on the fir-twig mattress before the fire she had kindled, and helped myself to the nice roast steak of venison, or the smoking fish she had prepared. And thus time passed, and I felt no inclination to regret that I did not keep Christmas that year at home in the far-off East. The blaze of the pine logs lit up for me Christmas-trees in the wild forest which seemed to me fairer than any I had helped to delight the children with at home. Our candles amid the branches were only the sparks ascending fitfully and dying in the green boughs, through which every here and there toward the outer fringes peeped the stars of the clear frosty heavens. My lodge of cedar and spruce bark, hung around a stack of sturdy young tree poles, was as smart and good as any in the camp. I had a store of smoked fish, and venison strips for all contingencies. I had deerskins, and furs from the bodies of some bears we had slaughtered, beautifully cured by Kiooshka, and on these I sat and smoked the pipe of contentment.

Then came entanglements of a yet more formidable character. I had gone with two Indians on a hunting expedition. One of these men was a decided admirer of Kiooshka's, and although she seemed to give him no encouragement, he had been looked upon as her affianced husband. This worthy young Brave naturally disliked me, and I saw him sullenly contemplating me often enough. He and the other had been no choice of mine as companions that day, but I had started with a rifle, and they had followed the same path I had taken. After a while, in a thicket of cedar, we came upon traces of moose. By this time the ill-disposed Mistusu, Kiooshka's friend, only was with me. The other man had diverged from us, and we had not seen him for three hours or more. I had not expected to have much sport, and had only taken three cartridges with me loose in my pocket. In following the game I stumbled more than once, and it must have been then that I lost these spare cartridges. But my rifle was loaded, and looking amid the boughs heavily laden with snow, I heard a rush, and saw a dark object for a moment. I raised my rifle and fired, and struggling through the dense and snow-laden boughs of evergreen I came on blood marks, and eagerly tracked them. In about half an hour I came up to a fine bull moose, whose horns were alone at first visible, for the animal was lying down in a little gully. I stopped for a moment to recharge my rifle, and found to my consternation that my few spare cartridges were gone. I pulled out my knife, and rushed on, and as I did so, and when near the moose, he regained his legs, lowered his head, and charged like a Spanish bull. I leaped on one side, but too late to avoid a sweep of his broad antlers, which wounded me in the leg, and threw me on one side. But it was his last effort. He reeled and fell, and I found that my bullet had been well planted behind the shoulder.

I shouted to the Indian, but he was nowhere to be seen. I now felt my leg very painful, and I dragged myself with difficulty out of the gully, and shouted again through the glades of the woods. There was no answer. Whether the Indian was watching me or not, I never knew. I felt the greatest distrust of Mistusu. I don't think I should have minded Kiooshka's marrying some Indian at this period, but I certainly did dislike very much the idea of her marriage with Mistusu. Now, however, I thought little of Kiooshka, and I shouted again for Mistusu. I certainly could not carry off any meat from the carcase without him, and I doubted, so great was the pain in my leg, which was now all swollen and blue if I could get home without him. It was no joke to be benighted in this lame condition, and I shouted and shouted again. There was no reply. Fortunately I had matches with me. I felt in my pockets for them, and they were there, all right. This relieved me of any very serious apprehension, for I thought that I could surely make my way back slowly, and I should not perish with the cold. A fire could always be made, and Kiooshka or the old man would send men on our track.

But time was slipping on, and I determined to make the most of what daylight remained. But my progress was pitifully slow, and the pain was so great that I found I was sweating as if in the tropics with the exertion of hobbling back on the track I had so swiftly made in the morning. At last I could bear it no longer; I exerted my remaining powers of locomotion to get material for a fire, which I accomplished with much trouble, and lay down before my little pile of wood, and husbanding it carefully, scraped away the snow and lit a small fire, keeping the remainder to prevent its dying out. My sleep was very broken, my wounded leg hurting me greatly.

As soon as it was dawn I crept on, and when nearly exhausted, saw to my joy Kiooshka with some of her people coming towards me. They lifted me and bore me back to camp, where Kiooshka became my ministering angel. My hurt was much inflamed, and she came to me with a white decoction of some species of bark, and made signs to me to bathe it. Never was there a more effective lotion. But movement was evidently impossible for some time. The horns of the powerful animal had torn the muscles and sinews, and some time must elapse before the limb could get whole. The white medicine had alleviated the pain, and nature would do the rest in time. I groaned in bitterness of spirit at this, the end of my sporting expedition. But Kiooshka seemed by no means unhappy. I asked after Mistusu, but my nurse only shook her head.

One morning the back doorway was darkened by an uncouth figure, the form of an Indian medicine man "got up," as we would say, "in full canonicals." He had come to heal me, I supposed; but I was weak and nervous, and this hideous figure seemed to me a nightmare. On its head were two horns, and strings of feathers depended from them around his head and breast. His face was concealed by a mask of some kind of white fur, leaving little visible. A white squirrel or some small animal had been used for this purpose; and there were odd tags and rags of all sorts of cloth and beads and feathers all about the figure, which came dancing and gibbering up to where I was lying, bending over me, and making strange incantations. He raised my head and put something to my mouth, and, although I had no doubt the action was well meant, I had strength enough to dash away the ill-smelling stuff which had been held under my nostrils — and then I looked at the bedizened face, and I thought I recognised Mistusu! I called aloud, and Kiooshka entered. As soon as she saw the figure she ran to us, and uttering cries, and what seemed to me to be energetic but still ladylike imprecations, she pushed the figure aside, and followed it with maledictions as it disappeared again through the doorway. Her anxiety about me was evident. She picked up the birch cup that had been presented to me, smelt it, and turned it round, and then went to the door and threw it away, and with signs and a great outflow of words made me understand that I was to have nothing to do with it. I said "Mistusu?" and she nodded and jabbered with a volubility that astonished me, for I had never seen her yield to excitement before.

Whether I was right or wrong I know not, but I imagined she had saved my life, and I took her hand and drew her towards me and kissed her, feeble as I was; and thereafter she seemed to be incessantly watching over me. She allowed no one but herself to see me, and tended me with the jealousy of a woman, and the devotion of a friend. I confess that I found myself longing for her presence, and fretful at her absence. My limb became less sensible of its injury, and I walked a little, and sat trying to make Kiooshka understand my mixture of Cree and English. I began to think that life with her in the woods would be very tolerable; but then came the recollection of marriages which had been made by white men with Indian demoiselles, and how I had always seen that the man seemed to descend to the woman's level, rather than the woman be elevated to the man's. To be sure there were exceptions, and was it not only because the man had not given the woman a fair chance that she had not improved? Why should she, and how could she improve, unless she

lived with white people? In the cases I
had known, the man had lived almost
entirely with the Indians, or at least by
himself with his Indian wife. Yet I had
known men happy enough, although they
were men as well educated as I was. I
remembered seeing a white baby in a lodge,
and asking whose it was, and had found it
belonged to a young engineer from Ontario
who had married a fine-looking squaw.
"That beb's half Injun and half engineer,"
was the observation, and Mrs. Engineer
seemed a happy enough wife. "Better
fifty years of . Europe than a cycle of
Cathay," I quoted to myself; but Canada
might be better than old Europe and Cathay
put together. Oh, Kiooshka, how weak is
man, even though he be a Toronto lawyer!
Meanwhile, the only decided proposition I

made to her was that she should cease to put a vermilion line down the parting of her hair, for this she was apt to do when she desired to please me most, as well as a little red lead rouge on her cheeks. That I did not like this rather hurt her, I fear, but I thought her appearance decidedly improved without the vermilion. She never wore it after I had shown her I liked her best without it. There was nothing else that was artificial about her. She never wore a bird's cage in the small of her back, as do the Toronto belles, nor did she ever comb her fine black hair over an old sponge, to make a glossy bunch at the back of her head. All round she was natural and well-shaped, and, as I thought, a very dear little girl. Her teeth were positively beautiful; this nobody could

deny. Her voice was pleasant, her expression charming, her helpfulness most
laudable. Her dependence on my appro-
bation was most flattering, and, as I
thought also, most natural. She could
quickly be taught anything—of this I was
positive. One day I made her put up her
hair in our fashion, and certainly she looked
very well. I told her so in my best Cree,
and she was enchanted. Oh, those pleasant
days, how soon to be ended !

She told me one evening that she had
seen a deer close to the camp. " Would I
like to come and kill it ? " Yes, I was
quite well and willing enough, and we
were off, wending our way cautiously and
slowly, and as noiselessly as possible. We
had got deep into the woods when the
deer was shown to me by her. I fired,

E

and she and I ran forward to the dying
deer. As we were standing close together
over the body, she took my hand in hers
and said, simply, "Saké ittan." "I love
you." What could I do? I kissed her!
The next moment—"S-s-s-s-t—thud," an
arrow shot just over my shoulder, and
struck her full in the chest. She gave
one long cry and fell. I was frantic.
Turning sharp round, I fired desperately
into the bush, where I imagined the enemy
to be. Then I flung myself down by her
side. To pull out the arrow seemed
impossible and useless. There it was,
imbedded in her heart. The next moment
she had drawn her last breath.

I rushed back to camp, and loudly,
furiously accused Mistusu, for I felt sure
it was he who had shot at me, and had

killed her. All was consternation, but the old Chief and head men were calm and silent. I led them to the body. Where was Mistusu? I demanded him—I swore to kill him. I know not what I said, for I raved. We bore her back to camp. I felt heartbroken. Mistusu had disappeared. Woe betide him, if I met him again. I could not stay in that place any more. I journeyed hurriedly to Carlton Fort, and there bidding good-bye with tears to the two Indians who accompanied me, and to whom I felt as to dear brothers, I took a dog team. Travelling as fast as these could take me by the known route to Portage le Prairie and Fort Garry, I arrived, worn out and harassed in mind and body, at that place. It was not till the spring had again clothed the plains around with grass, and the lakes were again alive with wild-fowl, that I thought of proceeding eastwards. But at last I made up my mind to plunge again into my old life, and found my Toronto friends greeting me as if I had only just left them. Yet to me years seemed to have passed. Many years did pass before fate again called me from my busy avocations in our Queen City.

But there came again a time that recalled to me all the bitterness of the days whose story I have narrated.

CHAPTER IV.

THE Half Breed Insurrection in the North-West broke out. Riel, who had made mischief in 1871, was again in the field, and was again hatching rebellion, not this time in his old quarters, but far away in those regions I knew too well. There his countrymen, the "Metis," had taken it into their heads that "Les Anglais" would interfere with their possessions, which were usually, as in French Canada, elongated slips of land, having a frontage on the Saskatchewan, and stretching back into the country behind.

The English, they said, would "square" these lands and interfere with their tenure. It was a false idea and could easily have been removed. But they were not reassured in time. They had arms, and got more, with some ammunition. Riel came at their invitation from the States, and it was evident that mischief was meant. Already some of the Indians had joined their Half Breed kinsmen.

I had been for some time an enthusiastic member of one of the Toronto Militia regiments. We were ordered up to "the front," as we already called the scene of impending trouble. But how different was this journey from that I had last undertaken to the North-West. Now we were regularly "entrained" in the splendid cars of the Canadian Pacific Railway, and we

reached without much trouble the city of
Winnipeg, now grown into a fine town,
and very different from the tumble-down
village I remembered. The greatest heartiness
was shown by the troops. At that time
there were some breaks in the line north
of Lake Superior, and we had to march a
bit through disagreeable slushy snow and
ice, for the spring was coming. Nothing
could discourage for a moment the high
spirits of our men. This was made very
apparent when we left the rail, and began
a very tedious and toilsome march over the
trail I had years before passed over in mid-
winter with my dog team. The food was often
insufficient, and the hardship from cold and
wet great. But onward we went, all longing
to be doing what we could to justify the
proud name of the Canadian Militia.

While the main body, after arriving in the neighbourhood of the south branch of the Saskatchewan, were turned towards Batoche, a name soon to become only too famous for the desperate fight which took place there between our men and the enemy, who were in numbers not inferior, and had all the advantages of position; I was one of a smaller force which was directed further to the west, to prevent a number of Crees and others from joining the rebels.

Carlton Fort was again reached, but we found it in ruins; it had been burnt by the enemy. How strange it seemed to me to be here again, with a number of red-coats, and with a strength great enough, as we believed, to carry all before it! But want of regular supplies of food told to some extent on the men, and we marched on, grumbling but resolute, until another stockaded fort on the river, named Battleford, was reached. Here we were comfortable enough. The long swelling lines of the bare prairie looked cheerless enough, but there was the great shallow stream still rolling past us in the vast hollow it had scooped for itself during the course of ages in the gravels and alluvial sands of the plains. A river always makes a landscape more interesting. Here, too, on the Battle River, which joins at this place the Saskatchewan, was a village among poplar groves. This had been looted by Indians, who, we were assured, had taken the war-path. Well, they should have a taste of our lead and steel! We had with us men of the Mounted Police — a gallant corps — well mounted, and accustomed to Indian manners, whether hostile or friendly. We had the brave Short, the *beau ideal* of an artillery officer, who would have been an ornament and credit to any service, and was the pride and darling of our own.

We heard that Poundmaker, a Cree, who had but lately acted as a guide to the Governor-General when he travelled hence to the Blackfeet, at the foot of the distant Rocky Mountains, had joined the rebels. This seemed to show that the hostile movement must be pretty general, for this man was an intelligent Indian, who had been much among the Blackfeet natives, as well as a leader among the Crees. Our leader determined to prevent these men under Poundmaker from joining Riel, to the westward; and as we had good information from our scouts, we left Battleford with a Gatling gun, two 7 lb. guns, 45 waggons, and about 150 men.

We halted at night until the moon rose, and then marched southwards all night, across long, swelling plains, with here and there a higher hill, and many clumps of poplar, growing especially in the little ravines. At daybreak we were near the Indian camp. Our guns opened with shrapnel as soon as the enemy was felt. Their fire was brisk, and our men suffered a good deal, their zeal causing them to expose themselves too freely. I was near Short, who, with Rutherford, was directing the fire of the guns. Short, as our leader (Colonel Otter) afterwards said, seemed to have a charmed life, as he coolly stood in the front lines working his guns. The action was very sharp, and it was difficult to see the enemy's sharpshooters, hidden as they were in the brushwood.

While I was watching a severe contest on my left, I heard some one shout: "Look out there — look at those fellows," and I saw a party of many Indians in the bush close to us. They came quickly, making a rush for the Gatling. In an instant, Short, with his revolver and sword drawn, had called us to him, and following him we rushed at the enemy. I remember only seeing Short's light forage cap lifted on his head by a shot that passed through it, and then I saw him hand to hand with the Indians, shooting one and rushing for another, who fired at him but missed. The Indian fell, a war-whoop on his lips. We fired and fired, and the enemy ran. I stopped for a moment at the body of the Indian who had fired last at Short. What face was that, now pale, and gasping forth blood from the lips? It was Mistusu! Here we had met again. I had but time to tear away his headgear. In the excitement I should like to have looted all his savage frippery, but we had to rush back to the Gatling. Then occurred more fighting, and it was not until some time later, that we found we had done what we could in breaking the enemy's march westward, and in giving them a lesson, and that our small force was not able to do more. We limbered up the guns with great difficulty, and retired slowly, the gun-trails having been broken and difficult to move. Short, ever at the post of danger, was the last to go, ever giving a return fire to the sharp pinging of the enemy's bullets. They did not pursue us, and we reached Battleford in good order, carrying all our dead but one.

I need not pursue the story of our brief campaign and victory. I do not desire more Indian experiences, either in love or war. Our successes were dearly achieved, and a good lesson was afforded by the outbreak to the Canadian Government, that lesson being that the rôle of the soldier is one that must be played even among the most peaceful and peace-loving people, and that it is folly not to have at all times a force well organised for defence, or the necessary offence which is the safeguard of defence.

If Canada had had more troops regularly enrolled, the outbreak would have been impossible. If she had recognised earlier the necessity that peace must be guarded by armed men in good array, she would not have had to deplore the doubtful battle of Cutknife, or the heavy losses at Batoche.

My tale is told, and although I say that my Indian experience has been quite enough for me, I am still in Canada's militia, although I do carry about in the Law Courts the blue bag which is the badge of the enterprising barrister. I began with some moral reflections on the regret that does not always accompany silly actions. I hope Canada, as a whole, will be wiser than I, a humble Canadian individual. Although long since happily married, I do not regret either my acquaintance with poor Kiooshka or having been "in at the death" of Mistusu.

TO BE, OR NOT TO BE

TO BE, OR NOT TO BE

By MRS. ALEXANDER

"DID you ring, mem?"

The question was addressed by a tall, angular, hard-featured, elderly woman, in an old-fashioned black stuff dress, a large snow-white apron, and an equally white cap, closely befrilled in bygone style, to a lady not unlike herself —but older, slighter, whiter, and gentler in aspect—who, clothed in black silk, with a gray Shetland shawl round her shoulders, and a cap of delicate lace on her carefully curled white hair, sat by a small fire.

"I did, Janet. Will you attend to the fire? It hurts my back to stoop."

"And why should ye? You are aye too ready to fash yoursel'."

As she spoke the elderly servant knelt down and proceeded to add a few lumps of coal, with much caution, to the dying embers, covering them with the best cinders she could pick from the hearth, which she swept up, and striking the brush against the bars, to shake off the dust, hung it up again.

"Has Miss Ayton returned yet?"

"No."

"She is very late," said the old lady, querulously; "she needn't take two hours to buy half a shoulder of mutton and two pounds of potatoes."

"Hoot toot, mem. It's a fine bright

morning. What for shouldn't a fine young lassie like Miss Olive tak' a turn round about? Ye ken she is kepit pretty close i' the house."

"She has much more liberty than young leddies have in general," returned her mistress, sitting very upright. "For all the twenty years I was companion and secretary to the Marchioness of Glencairn, I never once knew the Leddies McCallum go out alone."

"Eh! then they might have walked round the world, any one of them, an' naebody give a second look at their reed heeds! What for should ane sort o' girlie be so sair looked after, and anither just let to face a' the dangers of life alane?"

"Janet, for a Christian woman, you are a sad democrat!"

'"For a Christian, mem? Weren't Christians the first democrats of a'? But I hear the gate," stepping sharply to a little bay-window. "Yes, it's herself and Amanda wi' the basket! Eh! of all the untidy taupies, yon girl's the worst! There's half a yard of the braid from her dress streeling behind her."

"Send Miss Ayton to me," called her mistress, as she was leaving the room; "I want to give her her letter."

She took up the letter which lay on a little work-table beside her and turned it over, studying the post-marks and evidently much exercised by its aspect.

While she looks and ponders, an explanatory word.

Miss Tabitha Drummond, of Hazelwood Villas, Notting Hill, was a Scotch gentlewoman of good family — indeed a remote kinswoman of that Marchioness of Glencairn, so well known for her works of benevolence and missionary enterprises, and who — in spite of her supposed boundless charities— had left a tolerable fortune, on which a small annuity was charged in favour of the faithful companion who for years had been an almost unpaid *attaché*. This, with the interest of a small sum inherited from a relative, enabled the good spinster to live with great economy and some comfort in a tiny house all her own, with her faithful follower, Janet, erst school-room maid in the great Glencairn establishment.

Here, when the last summons called her half-brother, the Rev. John Ayton, from his work as vicar of Netherly, she received his orphaned, penniless daughter, Olive —

albeit by no means friendly with the deceased, who had forsaken the Kirk and taken holy orders in that semi-Romanist institution, the Church of England, and was altogether too much of a Southern.

The girl had been petted and somewhat spoilt. She had never been sent to school, and though by no means ignorant, had not been fitted to earn her bread. The poor vicar had invested his little all in a tempting scheme, which smashed according to its kind — his last hours being embittered by the knowledge that his young daughter was left unprovided for. Then he turned to his estranged sister, and she did not fail him.

Miss Drummond had laid down the letter again, when the door opened, and her niece entered—a tall, slender, willowy-looking girl, with nut-brown hair, and dark eyes of no particular colour, but somewhat sad when she neither spoke nor smiled. She had pale cheeks, but red lips, and a rather wide but sweet mouth, a little suggestive of kind words and kisses.

"Did you want me, auntie? I only stayed to give the things to Janet. I ventured to buy a little seakale, for I know you like it."

"I am afraid you are a wasteful bairn —but come your way. Here is an Indian letter for you!"

"Ah! How good of Selina to write so soon again!"

"It's not from Selina Prendergast! 'Sialkot' is the name in the post-mark, and it's a man's writing; so be frank with me, niece. What man in India has the right to address a letter to you?"

"What man?" repeated Olive Ayton,

with a tone of frank surprise in her soft,
fresh voice. " I cannot imagine what man
could write to me ! I don't think I have
spoken to one since my dear father died
—except that dreadful scholastic agency
creature. I am sure you are welcome to
see it, Aunt Tab ! " With another specu-
lative look at its exterior, Olive opened
the envelope, and proceeded to read the
letter enclosed, her eyes growing rounder
and more surprised as she proceeded.
Finally, with a sudden sigh of astonishment,
she exclaimed : " Horace C. Barclay ! How
extraordinary ! Did you not know something of him, auntie ? "

" Yes, of course I did. I gave him and
his cousin an introduction to your father
when they went into country lodgings to
study, years and years ago. The cousin

was a wiselike laddie — but he's dead, poor fellow! What is it all about, my bairn?"

"Read it yourself, auntie. I am afraid Horace is not as 'wiselike' as his cousin."

Miss Drummond put on her spectacles, and read in a sort of unconscious whisper:

"I wonder if my dear, sedate little Olive —my playfellow of nearly ten years ago— remembers the uncouth medical student who used to tease her, even to tears, during his pleasant visits to Netherly Vicarage? If she does, I fear the impression left on her memory is by no means delightful! Yet, in spite of this conviction, I am going to do what almost every one would declare was foolish, if not insane. Let me say a few words about myself before I avow my folly. I bade good-bye to you, and to the only bit of life that ever gave me the faintest idea of home, a day or two before starting for India, and here I have been ever since, very busy, and not unsuccessful. Many a time I have sat in the balmy evening air, and the silence of some remote station, and thought of you and your good father. I wrote to him once, but never had a reply, so I thought he did not care to hear more of me, and many absorbing matters connected with my profession pushed the past out of my mind.

"About a month ago I was down at Umballa, and there I met Colonel Prendergast, who invited me to his bungalow, and, conversing with his wife, I found that the old Squire at Netherly was her father, and that one of her daughters was your especial friend. They told me that the good vicar was dead—that you had to leave your sweet home and struggle among strangers, as my former patroness, Miss Drummond, could not keep you always under her wing; they showed me your photograph, and I could scarcely refrain from making an ass of myself, and kissing it before them all! Then a passionate wish to take you in my arms, and take care of you always, sprang to life in my heart, and set my pulses beating! A day or two after I returned to the regiment here, and found a letter offering me an appointment I had been long anxious to gain, on the Medical Staff at G——. I resolved at once to take eighteen months' leave to go home, to offer myself to you, and risk a snubbing if you were so disposed. Now don't think me presumptuous. You may be married by the time I reach England —you may be engaged; if so, why, give my best wishes to your husband or your *fiancé*, and tell him if he makes you happy, I'll be proud to be his friend. If you are still free and heart-whole, don't refuse me right away, give me a chance, and if I am so lucky as to win you, I'll try with all my heart and soul to make your life as fair and smooth as it was in the old days. Am I a fool to write all this? God knows! Anyhow, I'll stick to it. I cannot resist the impulse that prompts me. I have your address from Miss Prendergast, and I hope to be in London almost as soon as my letter — so good night, sweet little friend! Will you ever be more?

"Your sincerely attached,

"Horace C. Barclay.

"P.S.—I shall put up at Morley's, Charing Cross."

"My patience!" ejaculated Aunt Tabitha, handing the letter to its owner. "Did any one ever know the like? Nay, he is *not* wiselike; but for all that, I can see a direct Providence in yon letter, only I'm thinking that if you two agree together, it's but small common-sense ye'll have between ye —it's what you're very deficient in, Olive; and for this young man——"

"He is — he must be rather crazy," interrupted Olive, who was smiling as she re-read her letter. "Why, he may not like me when he sees me! and I—I had nearly forgotten him. He was a dreadful tease, and a great, long, bony creature, with wild black hair. But he was kind. I remember when I slipped and sprained my ankle, how he carried me home; but to marry him—that is a very serious matter."

·"Ay! a very serious matter indeed
Olive Ayton! You must just look on it
as the workings of a Divine Providence.
Here you have been three months looking
for an engagement, and never one offered.
Even if it did, what would you get? Five-
and-twenty pounds a year at most — you
had but twenty besides your keep at Mrs.
Kerrmudgeon's, and you had three girls to
teach—for-bye th' rudiments o' Latin to two
boys! Your education has been sore neglected. You never acquired French in
Paris, your arithmetic is just woful, and
you have never passed an examination of
any kind. Then you have no style in
your composition. Do you think my late
kinswoman, the Marchioness of Glencairn,
would have put up with me for twenty-
seven years as her companion and ama-

nuensis, if I had not had some elegance of style in my letter-writing?"

"I am sure I dread another engagement, if I am to meet with a second supply of Kerrmudgeons," said Olive with a sigh. "I know I am too ignorant to teach, except quite little children. I would far rather go out as lady's-maid. I love handling pretty clothes, even if they are not my own—only you would be ashamed of me, Aunt Tab."

"I would be! I *am* ashamed of you for your want of proper pride! Now the Lord has shown you an honourable way out of the drudgery you dislike so much. Here is an honest man ready to take you — and it's not many that would take a penniless lass — with or without a 'lang pedigree' — so you make up your mind, and when you meet this well-meaning laddie, just accept him with all due dignity and consideration, and you'll have an easy life of it."

"Don't be too sure of that, auntie. From all I see, most married lives are exceedingly *uneasy*. If I could like Horace Barclay it would be very nice, but if I cannot, why, the last state of this young person," tapping her bosom, "would be a good deal worse than the first."

"Don't quote Scripture in a disrespectful spirit, Olive Ayton. Once ye have the minister's blessing and feel you are pledged for life, a proper degree of affection would spring up——"

"Or an improper degree of dislike,' returned Olive, thoughtfully.

Miss Drummond continued to utter much

admirable and religious sense, but somehow it did not penetrate to Olive's understanding. She somewhat abruptly interrupted the flow of her aunt's eloquence by saying she must go and take off her hat and jacket.

In the retirement of her own room she read over more than once the startling letter she had just received — read it with blushing cheeks and moist eyes. Its kindly, generous tone touched her heart. This man only asked to give her everything, and seemed to look on her acceptance of his affection as a favour. She quickly began to hope she *could* love him. Perhaps he had grown less angular and wild-looking; she would like to make *him* happy and comfortable. *If* he were nice and sympathetic, how lovely life might be! She seemed suddenly to realise how hard it was at present. The stern necessity of working for herself, of relieving her aunt from the cost of her maintenance, compelled her in self-defence to shut her eyes to much that she dreaded.

The rest of the day passed over in a dreamy condition. Aunt Tabitha talked and drew pictures of the future, but Olive silently plied her needle — and heard her not. And when night came, Horace Barclay might have had reason to hope, could he have known the innocent yet disturbing visions which visited his sleeping love.

CHAPTER II.

A WEEK had passed over in a curiously slow yet rapid way, at least to Olive. · To her aunt it went fast indeed. She had the whole house cleaned and put in order, fresh muslin curtains were hung up, and as the last extremity of preparation sundry bottles of superior Highland whisky were ordered by Miss Drummond, from the famous firm that formerly supplied her revered patroness, Lady Glencairn.

Thus armed at all points, Aunt Tabitha sat down with a quiet conscience to await the arrival of her niece's future husband, as she determined Dr. Barclay should be.

It was rather late in the afternoon, and Olive was busy with her needle as she sat beside her aunt's work-table, occasionally forcing herself to talk in order to resist the thoughts which haunted her, when the sound of a carriage stopping, with an immediate loud peal at the front-door bell, made her heart leap and then stand still.

" Goodness ! " said Miss Drummond, laying down her patchwork. " It can't be——" She looked anxiously at her niece. It was not necessary to finish her sentence. Olive knew what she meant, and growing very white, exclaimed :

" Oh, no ! It would be impossible."

To them enters Janet, upright and grim, with a card.

"It is," ejaculated Aunt Tabitha, and read aloud, "Dr. H. C. Barclay." "Ask the gentleman to step up, Janet."

Olive rose, feeling she could scarcely stand. The next moment Dr. Barclay was greeting her aunt. Could this be the tall, lanky, frolicsome Horace she had known ? Yes ; the features, the height, the bold black eyes, the abundant black hair, all were the same, but—— He had grown stout, very stout ; his massive, fleshy shoulders gave him the air of being short-necked ; his somewhat puffy cheeks made his eyes look small and piggish. He was well and fashionably dressed ; well groomed from head to foot ; certainly good-looking—but so much older, so different from what she expected, that her heart sank. Meantime Dr. Barclay was greeting her aunt with a kind of blunt assurance, by no means pleasing to Olive's fastidious taste.

"How d'ye do, ma'am? Glad to find you looking as well as ever. Lost no time in coming to see you. Only arrived yesterday. Got your address from Prendergast, son-in-law of the old Squire at Netherly."

"You are exceedingly good, Dr. Barclay, to call so soon on a lonely old woman. I assure you, you are most welcome."

"Thank you, thank you." The doctor was slightly short of breath, and puffed a little. "So this is my old friend, Olive" —putting out a large fat hand—"grown up a deuced pretty girl, by Jove! Hope you are glad to see me, too, Miss Olive—as I suppose I must call you?"

"Oh, yes; an old friend is always welcome!" murmured Olive, vaguely.

"That's right!" looking round uneasily for a seat strong enough to bear his weight.

"Try this," said Olive, perceiving his difficulty, and drawing forward a solid oaken arm-chair—the one *pièce de résistance* in the room.

"Ah! thanks! the very thing," said the doctor, taking it and depositing his beautiful new glossy hat on the carpet. "So you have left the Vicarage? Nice jolly old place. Never tasted better stout or finer home-brewed than at your poor father's. I was awfully cut up when I heard of his death—though he wasn't a young man, you know. I'd give him sixty-three."

"My late brother was sixty-five at the time of his decease," said Miss Drummond, a little stiffly.

"Ah! Indeed. Didn't marry young, I suppose?" continued the doctor, still addressing Olive. "And quite right, too! I have no patience with the boys who rush into matrimony nowadays. They should wait, as I have done, to be in the prime of life! I begin to think it's time to look out for a wife to take back with me. A fellow is awfully alone in India—one gets sick of always dining in uniform and boots—often tight boots—day after day."

"Why don't you wear easy ones?" asked Olive, who was rallying from her dismay, largely assisted by her sense of the ridiculous.

"Hey?" returned the doctor. "Why? Why, you see the fellows in London send you out a pile of boots in a box — deuced natty, and all that, but they forget the effect a tropical climate has on the extremities.

You see my hands. I used to take sevens when I went out first, and now I take eights and a half—give you my word I do. But you haven't told me what the poor vicar died of."

"He took a chill, going to see a parishioner—an old labourer, who——"

"Ay, it's just like those sort of people. I find no patients half so selfish and inconsiderate as paupers — think no more of having you out of your bed in the dead of the night for nothing than if they were ready with a five-guinea fee."

"Death, too, is very inconsiderate respecting times and seasons," said Olive, gravely.

"Gad, you've hit it," returned the doctor, seriously, by no means affected by her tone or words. Then, turning to Aunt Tabitha: "You are a good bit older than your brother, I fancy, but you look hale and well. I have always remarked that Scotchwomen are remarkably tough."

"The Scotch have remarkably good health, if that's what you mean," returned Miss Drummond, rather severely.

"Exactly. Now, Miss Olive, I expect you to lead me about. I haven't seen a play for years — I'm uncommon fond of a play if it's funny and makes you laugh. I suppose you'll not mind coming to the theatre with me?"

"There is no reason why she should; at any rate, I do not see any," remarked Miss Drummond, unbending.

"You are very good," cried Olive, colouring. "But our tastes would not agree; I only like plays that make me cry."

"And you call that amusing yourself!"

said the doctor, with a laugh; then addressing Miss Drummond: "I have brought you
a present, ma'am, from Miss Prendergast—
a deuced troublesome concern, I can tell
you. It's a Persian kitten. I didn't bring
it with me to-day; I wasn't sure about
finding you. The chamber-maid is looking
after it; it's jet black, and considered a
beauty. If you like, I'll bring it up to-
morrow."

"I am much obliged to Miss Prendergast.
I shall be very pleased to have it. And
perhaps, Dr. Barclay, you will partake of
luncheon with us, at half-past one?" said
Aunt Tabitha.

"With pleasure; I shall be delighted;
in short, I am somewhat pressed for time,
and I shall be glad to have a longer talk
to-morrow. Then, Miss Olive, we'll settle

about the theatre. If I go and cry with you, you must come and laugh with me. Gad! I had no idea I should find you grown up into such a fine young lady! Do you remember how angry you used to be with me when I swung you too high in that swing under the lime-trees?"

"I don't think I do."

"That's too bad of you, Olive—come, you must let me call you Olive—why, you were only a baby when I knew you. Oh! by-the-bye," turning to Aunt Tabitha, "what's become of Dugald McCallum? He was in the 107th Highlanders—awful scamp."

"Lord Dugald McCallum was perhaps a little too high-spirit ed, but he was a brave soldier, and married an Indian Princess with a large fortune. They live chiefly on the Continent!"

"Yes, I know! She was a desperate darkie, and they say he gambled away most of her money, etc."

A little more gossip and he rose to take leave.

"To-morrow at 1.30, then, I'll bring the kitten, and try and make friends with you! By Jove, I don't think you have forgiven me that swing yet!" shaking hands with Olive. "Delighted to find you so well, Miss Drummond! Till to-morrow."

Olive went to the window and watched him depart in silence; then she turned, and meeting her aunt's eyes, which were fixed upon her with an inquiring glance, burst into a laugh, and, throwing herself into a seat, exclaimed:

"Oh, auntie! what a falling off is there!"

"I don't understand you, niece ! What have you to find fault with ? "

"Oh, I don't find fault. But could you imagine that stout, self-satisfied, prosperous-looking man—writing such—such a letter ? "

" He is a remarkably fine looking, sensible man—and will make you an excellent husband," returned Aunt Tabitha, with strong emphasis.

" He shall not be my husband !" cried Olive, resolutely ; "and I do beg and implore you," clasping her hands as she spoke, " never to allude to that unfortunate letter I intend to write him a few civil lines, saying I cannot accept his offer — very friendly, you know."

" Olive Ayton ! If you commit so rash an act," cried her aunt, tremulously, " I must, reluctantly, insist on your quitting my house! It is—yes—it's not delicate, or —or ladylike, to think much of a man's appearance. It is a distinct flying in the face of Providence to reject the mercies——"

The entrance of Janet, who handed a letter to Olive, interrupted her.

" It is from the Scholastic Agency," cried Olive, when they were alone, " and comes at the right moment. I shall be able to obey you. I am to be at the office on Tuesday, the 25th, at 10 a.m., to meet the lady principal of a preparatory school for boys, at Margate, who requires a governess for the junior class; salary, twenty pounds, no washing or travelling expenses. I am advised to go early, as the young ladies will be interviewed in the order of their coming, and a rush is expected. There is a brilliant chance. I need not marry Dr. Barclay, and I can quit your house——"

"Don't be too sure! How do you know you will be chosen out of the expected crowd?"

"That is true. Oh, how dreadful it is to be poor! But I do not want to live on you, auntie; you have little enough for yourself. Why — why did you ask that great staring man to luncheon? He will want no end of goodies."

She rose and left the room without waiting a reply, for she felt the tears she could not repress almost welling over.

It was a cruel disappointment, and she was ashamed it should be so. She did not know how the castles she could not help building had laid their foundations in her heart.

Home—with a kind, delicate, considerate

gentleman for a companion, instead of the ruggedness of school-life, its sordidness and uncertainty — could she be blamed for dwelling on a picture so fascinating in its contrast to the reverse? But, with all her tenderness, Olive possessed a certain backbone of resolution and self-respect. She could never dream of marrying a blunt, dull, uninteresting man like Dr. Barclay, and she must not mislead him; so she took her pen quickly, and wrote a nice civil little note, thanking him for his kind recollection of her, but avowing that, in consequence of circumstances she could not then explain, she could not accept his offer — and therefore hastened to enlighten him as to the true state of affairs as soon as possible. Then she put on her hat and went to post it herself.

"Now he will not come to luncheon to-morrow—and how angry and disappointed poor auntie will be! I am sure she and Janet are compounding curry in preparation for the feast; I can smell the frying up here," was her reflection when she regained her own room, after an hour's walk through the avenues and "groves" of the surburban neighbourhood. "I am sorry to disappoint auntie; she has been very good to me in her way."

CHAPTER III.

ALL the next morning Olive was tremulously watchful. Surely a note or a telegram would come, offering some excuse on the part of Dr. Barclay. But no! the hours slipped by and nothing came.

One o'clock struck, and Miss Drummond came into the room, inspecting the final arrangements of the table.

"It's all very neat and orderly," she said, in a tone of satisfaction, which rapidly changed to shrill disapproval. "My patience, Olive! are you going to sit down in that shabby black frock?"

"It's not so bad, auntie; and Dr. Barclay won't see what I have on."

"Now that is just a dishonest speech, niece! That man has a pair of sharp een. Why, I am going to change my—— Eh! but here he is," interrupting herself, and as a hansom stopped at the door, "I cannot be seen in my morning wrap."

Rushing from the room, she left poor, dismayed Olive to bear the brunt of the encounter. The next moment the doctor, big, burly, self-satisfied, joyous as ever, was shaking hands with her, while she could not control the vivid colour that would mount almost to the roots of her hair.

"How are you? Glad to have a word with you by yourself; you know, somehow,

I didn't think you were all right with me yesterday. Never mind. There's no reason why we shouldn't be fast friends, is there, now?"

"Oh, no; not at all!" cried Olive, eagerly, understanding that the worthy doctor accepted his dismissal, and was anxious to be on a kindly, brotherly footing. "I am quite delighted to be friends with you."

"That's all right; that's like a girl with no nonsense about her;" and he shook hands with her again.

"I've got the cat there in a basket; let's take him out."

"By all means."

Quite relieved at this turn of affairs, Olive went into the hall, where a hamper stood. The doctor produced a pocket-knife,

and cut the cords which tied it, liberating
a fine black kitten, adorned by a beautiful
bushy tail, who with much self - possession
yawned, stretched, and then sat down to
contemplate its new surroundings.

"What a beauty!" cried Olive, taking
it up.

"Be careful; the little brute bites and
scratches, and I am deucedly afraid of a
cat's scratches," said Dr. Barclay.

"It seems quiet enough. How delighted
auntie will be!" And Olive carried it into
the drawing-room and placed it on the
hearthrug, from which it soon started on
a tour of inspection.

"I suppose you don't go out much to
dances or concerts, or things of that kind,
hey?" asked the doctor.

"Never!" emphatically.

"Come, that's hard lines for a pretty girl like you. Now we understand each other, you won't mind doing a play with me?"

"Not at all; I shall be delighted."

"That's right. I'll settle about it with the old lady." The words had hardly passed his lips when Miss Drummond entered, and the few minutes before lunch were amply filled up by the reception of the kitten and comments on its beauty.

Luncheon was successful on the whole. Dr. Barclay approved the curry, and ate largely of it. He was not quite so unstinted in his praise of the beer, of which he was evidently a *connoisseur*, and when after some macaroni cheese, his glass was filled with sherry, Olive observed he did not finish it; still the guest of the day was evidently well pleased and did by far the greater part of the talking himself. He told a variety of amusing stories, chiefly illustrative of his own cleverness in avoiding dangerous situations, and shifting unpleasant responsibilities on other people's shoulders. He chuckled a good deal over his success in these manœuvres, and seemed quite impervious to some rather cutting remarks from Olive, for which Aunt Tabitha cast reproving glances at the delinquent.

"I suppose you never saw much of your cousin after you went out to India?"

"No, next to nothing. He was a reckless sort of fellow — went in for sport and all sorts of wild expeditions; don't do you a bit of good, you know—so——"

"Ah! just so! generally ends the same way!" interrupted Aunt Tabitha.

Then the doctor turned to Olive. "I will see if I can get places for to-morrow, and come up and tell you what I've done. Now I have a visit to pay at Putney—can't think what makes people live in these out-of-the-way places—I'd rather live up here, by Jove. Till to-morrow, then! I've paid you an awfully long visit — but you are so agreeable, you see. Give you my word! didn't know how to get away——"

"Now, Olive, you have done very well," said Aunt Tab, approvingly; "you may turn up your dainty nose, but you know you have an unusually good chance, and I am glad to see that, after all, you have some sense."

"Indeed, I have not, according to your idea!" said Olive, flushing. "I am afraid you will be very vexed with me, but wrote a line to him yesterday, explaining that I could not really have anything to do with him. Still he must be good-natured, for he said just now there was no reason why we should not be friends, so you see——"

"Olive Ayton," interrupted her aunt, "I did not think, whatever your faults, that you were a double-dealing taupie! It's plain yon doctor is a wiselike man. He is not going to take the first 'No' from a bit lassie that doesn't know her own mind!" cried Aunt Tabitha, greatly exercised. A few sharp speeches were then exchanged, and Olive had some difficulty in smoothing matters sufficiently to induce her aunt to ring for Janet, and show her the kitten.

The doctor showed no ill-feeling, nor did he seem to heed the decided rejection

he had received. He came the next day
to say he could not secure places for *Our
Boys* until Monday. On this occasion he
had two cups at afternoon tea, and proved
his appreciation of Janet's thin bread and
butter. He described accurately to both
ladies the treatment which he pursued in
the case of the General's youngest daughter,
who suffered the year before from an aggra-
vated attack of chicken-pox. Then finding
that Olive was going to visit Lady Twenty-
penny, a friend of her aunt's who lived in
Porchester Terrace, he offered to drive her
there in a hansom. Olive preferred walking,
whereupon, though he avowed his detesta-
tion of that exercise, the gallant doctor
offered her his escort.

Olive grew touchy. Her aunt was
probably right—this tiresome, egotistical, im-

pervious man looked upon her as a frivolous baby who would say "yes" to-morrow as readily as she said "no" yesterday—consequently she was by no means an amiable or sympathetic companion.

On Sunday the immovable doctor again appeared about tea-time with a fresh batch of stories, and when taking leave of Miss Drummond, exclaimed, as if with a happy thought: "I say! is there any reason why Miss Olive shouldn't take a bit of dinner with me at the 'Cri'?—deuced good dinners they give. I could call for her, you know, and—— Hey! what do you think?"

"It is a proposition I should not entertain from every one else," said Aunt Tabitha, with much dignity; "but considering that you are an old friend, and that I approve your very disinterested intentions, I do not object——"

"You must remember, I am not sure how long I may be kept at that scholastic bureau," said Olive, much annoyed by her aunt's speech.

"The what?" asked the doctor, with something of horror in his tone.

"An agency for obtaining engagements to teach—where I hope to find one," said Olive, steadily.

"Oh! Ah—yes, to be sure; well, do not let me interfere with your arrangements, only if you can be ready at six to-morrow, just drop me a line at my hotel—Morley's, you know—Charing Cross. Gad! it's past six now; I always pay you such awful long visits." With some haste he left them.

"I wonder he cares to come," said Olive.

"I feel less and less able to do the agreeable the longer I know him."

"And I wonder at it, too," returned Miss Drummond, solemnly; "you are be-having badly and foolishly, Olive. What made you talk about seeking an engagement and an agency office? Men like Dr. Barclay hate to hear of working women, or poverty; even though he might not ask money with you, he would not like to think you had come in contact——"

"He need not trouble himself," inter-rupted Olive. "What I am, or have been, or will be, does not concern him. Do not think about him any more, dear auntie; I have a sort of hope that Monday may bring me better fortune and you relief."

CHAPTER IV.

BUT [Olive's prophetic feeling was but a will-of-the-wisp—false and misleading.

The lady before whom the candidates for the magnificent appointment above described were paraded had selected one whose accomplishments, in the way of darning house-linen, turned the scale before it came to Olive's turn to enter the audience-chamber.

As she was rather dejectedly leaving the office, a lady was reading the various inscriptions which, in the usual way, adorned the entrance.

I

" I am looking for the Scholastic Agency Office," she said in a pleasant voice. " Would you be so good as to direct me ? "

" Certainly," returned Olive. " When you get to the first landing, turn along a passage to the left; at the end of it there is a dark, narrow stair. Stay, I will show you —it is a little complicated."

And Olive led her to the presence of the agent himself; a small, sallow man, with straggling beard and keen little eyes, who was pleased to be very peremptory with the humble seekers for employment thronging his office, and filling his pockets with their hard-earned shillings. As she left the dusty, dingy bureau, she heard the stranger ask, quickly :

" What is that young lady's name ? "

On reaching Hazelwood Villa, Olive found

her aunt sitting up very straight indeed, with her knitting in her hands, and severity enthroned on her brow.

"After all, auntie, I have not had any luck."

"No; I'm thinking you have thrown away your luck. Read that telegram," handing it to her.

It was addressed to Miss Drummond, signed H. C. Barclay, and contained these words: "Called out of town — important business—will write."

"There's an end of that, or I am much mistaken," she said, bitterly.

"I dare say it is. Oh, dear! how sorry I am not to see *Our Boys.*"

"Olive Ayton! I did not think you were a frivolous, light-headed young woman who would turn your back on the mercies o' Divine Providence, and disregard the counsels o' your only living kinswoman——" etc., etc.

And Aunt Tabitha scolded on, regardless of the fact that Olive had fallen into deep thought and did not appear to catch the sound of her words.

Dr. Barclay's business took him to see an old Indian acquaintance at Cheltenham; and as his absence from town hardly exceeded forty-eight hours, he did not find it convenient to write according to promise.

He reached town in time for his 7.30 repast, and making his way to the coffee-room, asked with some eagerness for the *carte*. He was studying its contents when another gentleman coming in, made the same demand, in a deep, commanding tone. The doctor looked up hastily, and gazed for a moment at the speaker. A tall man — very tall — and bony, even gaunt. He had a fine, strong, embrowned face, though by no means handsome, with re- markably dark, piercing eyes, thick black moustache, and abundant black hair, cut close at the back in military fashion. After an instant's hesitation, Dr. Barclay stepped forward, holding out his hand.

"By Jove! I did not expect to meet you here. Had no idea you were coming home."

They shook hands with some cordiality.

"Well, it was a rather sudden thought," replied the other; "but I fancied a whiff of native air would do me good, so here I am. Shall we dine together?"

"By all means—and, look here," seizing the *carte.* "They make capital calves' head hash, and let's have a duck — a pair of

ducks — and green peas, and a bottle of
Moselle — it's not bad here, give you my
word. Did you see Allan before you left?
He is a wonderful fellow — made such a
wonderful hit with the Commander-in-Chief
just before I started—tell you all about it
at dinner. Here, waiter, the wine *carte.*"

The lively doctor chatted eagerly through
dinner. It was evident from their talk that
they had many reminiscences and acquaintance in common, yet they were not especially
intimate friends; the new-comer was remarkably taciturn and frequently did not
seem to hear the abundant talk of his
companion. At last Dr. Barclay exclaimed:

"What's the matter with you, man?
Are you down on your luck? You don't
seem yourself! Liver—eh? Do you know,
I have invented a capital pill, with a dash

of mercury in it, which would put you right in a twinkling? I'm thinking seriously of patenting it. It is wonderful; old Sir Peregrine Pounceby, First Commissioner of Moolahbad, never stirs without a box of 'em in his pocket; give you my word!"

"Patent it if you like, but don't poison a brother practitioner," returned his friend, with a grim smile. "Fact is, England seems strange and cold to me. I went away a boy, I come back and find — nothing! I arrived yesterday morning, and yours is the first familiar face I have seen since. I'm thinking of going off to Paris on Saturday, to join Sir Arthur Dacre, the great *shikari*, you know! He is going into Hungary — the Carpathians — on a sort of exploring tour. There is nothing to keep me here."

"My dear fellow, London is a first-rate place! I am here barely a fortnight, and I have more engagements than I know how to keep. I've met lots of old friends, and— oh! I knew I had something to tell you! Do you remember the parson, down there at Netherly, where you were so fond of going to fish? Half-brother of that queer old Scotchwoman, the Marchioness's amanuensis — well, I found her out. The youngest Prendergast girl sent home a cat for her— and the devil's own bother I had with that infernal kitten. Well, Miss Drummond has old Ayton's daughter, little Olive, living with her; she has grown up an uncommon pretty girl — uncommon, by Jove! You remember the Vicarage, and your taking me there after you had been introduced yourself?"

The other nodded, and began to pull his long moustaches, and listen with an air of profound attention.

"Well, you see, though I am pretty wide-awake, I am no wiser, in some respects, than my neighbours, and I was immensely taken! She is such a shy, bright, sharp little puss! And I thought it would be deuced amusing to show her about a bit; she is awfully dull, you know, shut up with old Lady Glencairn's ex-secretary — they haven't a rap, give you my word! But the poor little girl took to me at once; I saw it was all up with her at the second interview. She was all blushes, tremors, and 'keep your distance' airs, that we understand, don't we, boy? Ha! ha! ha!" His listener made a sudden movement, and uttered a deep, inarticulate sound, which did

not seem exactly like a blessing. "She was
ready to walk with me, or talk with me,
or go to the play with me," resumed Dr.
Barclay. "I was always rather a favourite
with the women! Well, I had got places
for some confounded burlesque here in the
Strand, and thinking it would be an awful
bore to drive all the way up to their place,
to fetch my little girl after dining, I said to
Aunt Tabby: 'I suppose there is no reason
why Miss Olive shouldn't dine with me at
the "Cri," or "Verey's"?' What do you
think the old girl said? 'Considering you
are an old friend, and that I am aware of
your disinterested or honourable intentions,
I do not object'—give you my word, she
did! Now that expression 'intentions,'
brought me to my senses. It has a deuced
ugly sound, hasn't it? I just said I'd write

a line and say what hour I'd call for Miss Olive, but I found it wiser to be called out of town, ha? and I will just let them down easy! Take another glass of claret—it ain't bad, you see. Aunt Tabby knows that I am well up in the Service, and that I have a snug bit of house and other property, and I dare say she has imparted her knowledge to my pretty, tremulous, saucy little dove, so I mustn't let myself be victimised; a wife ought to have something more than——"

Here his listener, who had become rather restless, started from his seat, exclaiming rather inadvertently: "It's infernally hot! Suppose we take a stroll up Whitehall——"

"Don't move so soon after dinner! We have to finish that claret, too. But, I say, won't you go to see our friends?"

"No!" rather roughly. "They have forgotten me, I dare say. Did Olive — I mean Miss Drummond—ask for me?"

"Never mentioned your name, my dear fellow." No reply. "I tell you who did ask after you very kindly. Shirley! Don't you remember old Ayton's lantern-jawed curate? I met him in Cheltenham yesterday. He has a grand church there—is a popular preacher—wears a soft hat, white bands, and a coat to his heels. He was struck of a heap at seeing me, for it seems there was a report that I died of fever or something a couple of years ago. He asked after you, and said how pleased he'd be to see you again. He thought me so like you, only, of course, better filled out. It is a pity that nothing puts flesh on your bones."

"I prefer being as I am."

"Well, there's no accounting for tastes. Won't you come up and see little Olive Ayton? To tell you the truth, I want to see her myself, and I'd feel safer with you beside me."

"Nonsense, man. They don't want to see an insignificant fellow like me, who has no property at his back."

"As my relative you would be welcome," said Dr. Barclay, impressively. "Besides, you used to be the greater favourite of the two with little Olive."

"Ay, but little Olive was an unsophisticated little girl then."

"Well, she ain't bad now. It is only natural that a girl should try to get hold of a good-looking fellow with a decent property."

"Oh, very likely; at any rate, you are not such an ass as I am!"

"Well — perhaps not!" candidly and modestly.

"Besides," continued the other, "there is no necessity for my staying in this huge wilderness of bricks and mortar. I can do all I want to-morrow and run over to Paris. Now, Bertie, I don't know what you are going to do, but I am going out." So saying, he took down his hat and left the room.

"Beastly temper!" said Barclay to himself, complacently, "always had! Forgotten to pay for his dinner, too! But he'll put that right — he was always ready - enough with his cash!"

WHILE Dr. Barclay was thus entertaining his *convive*, the unconscious heroine of his narrative, Olive Ayton, who had been out nearly the whole afternoon, came in at her aunt's "high tea-time," looking much brighter than she had for some days.

"May I take off my hat here, auntie? I am rather hungry and very tired, and I have a great deal to tell you."

"Very well; and tell Janet to cook you an egg——"

"Oh, a little cold beef will do as well;"

and quickly laying aside her out-door gar-
ments, she set to work upon the food before
her.

"Well," asked Aunt Tabitha, when she
had waited a few minutes, "and what have
you to tell me?"

"After all," began Olive, with animation,
"last Monday was not so unlucky for me;
I have found an engagement, and not a bad
one, at last."

"You don't mean to say, Olive, that
you have finally accepted anything without
consulting me?"

"I was obliged, auntie, or I should
have lost it. Mrs. Buchanan, the lady who
asked me to call upon her, is the same
lady I met at the Agency Office, and she
seems rather to have taken a fancy to me."

"Buchanan, eh!—Scotch?"

" She is the wife of a Scotch minister somewhere in Perthshire; she offers me twenty-five pounds a year, and will pay my travelling expenses; she seems nice and kind, and said it was a very small salary, but she really could not afford more. She said, too, that if I were what I looked I might be happy with them. She has two girls and a boy—oh, and a baby. The boy is in bad health, and she is so much occupied with him that the girls are neglected; she wants me to travel with her on Saturday."

" What! without references on either side ? " asked Aunt Tabitha, aghast.

" Oh! she seemed satisfied with the agent's account of me, and gave me the address of the minister of that new Scotch church near the Royal Crescent."

" What! Mr. MacFarlane ? "

"Yes; so I called there before I came in, for I knew you would be in a fidget. Mr. MacFarlane seemed to know the family quite well, and spoke highly of both Mr. and Mrs. Buchanan."

"Olive, my bairn, you just take away my breath. Now if you start off on Saturday, how will you sort your clothes— and the doctor? What's to do about him?"

"He does not enter into my calculations —at all events, he will understand that my 'no' meant no, and there's an end of it. I fancy something we said or did when he was here last offended him. He went off so suddenly. I should not be surprised if we heard very little more of him."

"Hoot toot! my dearie, it's bare three days since he was here."

"Do not let us trouble about him, auntie; I want you to see that this is really a good chance for me. It is a long way from you, but I am not of much use."

Miss Drummond was not to be so easily persuaded into giving up her golden hopes of the doctor, and the discussion was continued with some heat on both sides, Olive at last wringing a reluctant consent from her disappointed aunt.

The day but one after was Friday, and Olive went by invitation to arrange the hour, etc., of their journey with her new employer. The minister's wife was staying with a relative in the wilds of Brixton, and kept her visitor a considerable time. It was therefore late when Olive alighted from an omnibus and attempted to cross the wide space at the top of Northumberland Avenue, which was much crowded. Twice she essayed to start, and twice she retreated; a third time she ventured, when a rough-looking man, with a heavy basket on his shoulder, pushed impatiently against her; her foot slipped on the pavement, which was damp and greasy, and she fell to the ground, almost under the feet of a horse, which was coming rapidly along in the shafts of a hansom. There was a scrambling and clattering of hoofs, as the driver strove with all his might to pull the animal on its haunches; a scream from the crowd, "She's killed! She's under the horse's feet!" and, with a sharp sense of pain added to her mortal terror, Olive became for a minute or two unconscious.

The gentleman who was in the cab

sprang from it in an instant, and had raised the half-fainting girl before the inevitable policeman could intervene.

" She's alive, and I hope she is not seriously hurt," he said to those nearest. " Is there a chemist's anywhere near? I am a surgeon, and will see to her."

A dozen voices directed him, and preceded by the solemn guardian of the law, who remained a sentinel at the door, the gentleman carried the injured girl to the druggist's indicated.

" Ah ! here's the mischief," he exclaimed, as Olive shrank from his · touch and moaned. " The left arm is broken; we must put that to rights at once; we must cut off the sleeve. Is there any woman about who could help us ?"

"Might I not go home first?" murmured Olive, faintly. She had come to herself, though feeling curiously dazed and bewildered, for the shock had been great.

"Your arm will come right all the sooner if we lose no time, and I have all appliances at hand here," returned the gentleman, who had apparently taken the command.

Here the owner of the shop, who had gone out, hastily returned with a stout, respectable-looking woman, his housekeeper, who, with many whispered exclamations of "Poor dear," "Bless her heart," "Ain't it cruel?" etc., snipped away the sleeve, and supported Olive's head, while the ex-occupant of the cab set the broken bone.

"Can you tell me where you live?" was his final question.

Olive, who again felt very faint, murmured her address, adding:

"My aunt will be frightened—and what shall I do about Mrs. Buchanan? I could not travel to-morrow, could I?"

"Most certainly not!" was the prompt reply. "Do not trouble about anybody—just try to get well." Then, turning to the chemist, he took from him some composing mixture. "Take this, and I shall see you safe home. The sooner you are in bed—after such a shock to the nervous system—the better."

Olive obeyed meekly.

"I rather think I know this young lady's relatives," said the surgeon to the owner of the shop. "If you send for a cab, I will take her home. There is my card; I am staying quite near, at Morley's."

It seemed to Olive that only two minutes elapsed before she was half lifted, half supported into a cab, where cloaks and cushions had been arranged for her comfort, and she was dimly conscious that for part of the way at least her head lay against her kind companion's shoulder.

She was next vaguely surprised to find Aunt Tabitha and Janet waiting in the hall, her own room ready and the bed turned down.

How thankful she was to be in it, and quite quiet! Then the local doctor, who did what healing Miss Drummond's small household needed, came and felt her pulse, and patted her in a fatherly fashion, assuring her she would be all right in a few weeks. How delightful it was to feel a drowsy sensation stealing over her, when her aunt left her, promising to write by the next post to Mrs. Buchanan.

Less than a week saw Olive greatly recovered, and able to come into the drawing-room, though still a little weak and tremulous. Every one had been so kind; their few acquaintances had brought her fruit and flowers; Mrs. Buchanan had come all the way from Brixton the very day on the evening of which she was to travel north, and offered to wait a month for her; and her aunt informed her Dr. Barclay had called every day. " Indeed," added that gentlewoman, " it's your own fault if you ever have to go looking for a living again," and she smiled knowingly.

"Auntie," cried Olive, "not a word about him, this first day of emancipation from my room."

"Well, well, I must e'en humour you, my bairn! You look wan and weakly enough," said Aunt Tabitha, kindly. Wan, but infinitely, delicately pretty, in her gray dressing-gown, the left sleeve opened up one seam and held together with bows of pink ribbon, a soft, fleecy Shetland shawl thrown round her, her dark gray, thoughtful eyes looking larger than usual, from the shade below them and the thinness of her pale face.

"And that kind, clever gentleman, who was so wonderfully good to me—I suppose

he is gone away? I remember, in spite of
my terror—for I thought my last hour had
come—that there was luggage, a portman-
teau, on the cab, as if he were going to
some train. It is curious, his eyes seemed
so familiar to me! You have never told me
his name."

"You see, dearie," Miss Tabitha was
beginning, when Janet opened the door.

"Here's the doctor—Dr. Barclay. Will
Miss Olive see him?" she asked.

"Oh! not to-day, auntie."

"Hush! my bairn," hastily; "he'll not
stay long—and—I'll go and tell him you
are not equal to much." She left the room,
leaving an impression on her niece's mind
that she was rather upset, an extraordinary
condition for Aunt Tabitha.

But the door opened again, this time to admit the tall, dark-eyed, sunburnt man who had succoured her so tenderly in her time of need.

"Oh! I am so glad to see you!" she cried, stretching out her right hand, while the colour sprang up in her cheek and gave light to her eyes; "I was afraid it was Dr. Barclay!"

"Poor Dr. Barclay!" he returned, with a smile, as he took her hand and kissed it gently. "What has he done? But first tell me how you feel. I trust you are not feverish," looking earnestly at her flushed cheeks, resisting for an instant her effort to withdraw her hand.

"I am quite well—wonderfully well," said Olive, feeling curiously confused; "and as to Dr. Barclay, he has only been very good-natured; but if you know him you will think with me that, for a person who is not very strong, Dr. Barclay is a little— a little overpowering."

"Perhaps so," sitting down on the sofa beside her.

"I am so glad to have an opportunity of thanking you," resumed Olive, shyly. "My arm would not have been nearly so well had you not set it at once—and—and you were wonderfully kind." There was a slight tremor in her voice.

"It makes me very happy to hear you say so," he returned in a low tone, leaning forward to rest his elbow on his knee, his chin in his hand, and turning to look into her eyes.

"Talking of Dr. Barclay," he resumed,

"I was more intimate with the other cousin, the one——" He paused.

"The one who died," put in Olive.

"Neither of them died."

"What do you mean? The elder—Hubert—died; my aunt told me so."

Her listener smiled and shook his head.

"I assure you that Hubert is quite well—as large as life, and reposing himself at this moment at Morley's Hotel, after a severe dinner yesterday at the house of a friend, an old civil servant."

"How extraordinary! That is where Horace Barclay is staying too."

"No, my dear little friend Olive, Horace Barclay is here beside you, to reproach you with your hasty dismissal before you gave him a chance."

"Ah!" exclaimed Olive—a long-drawn "ah." "That accounts for your eyes—I felt I knew your eyes. What an extraordinary mistake! How—how did it all happen?"

"It was the curious effect of a simple cause. Bertie—as we have generally called him—and I had not met for a considerable time; I had no idea he was coming to England. He stopped at Umballa, and was charged with the care of the kitten for Miss Drummond. His initials are the same as mine; he is Hubert Charles Barclay, I am Horace Carter Barclay. Believing Hubert to be dead (he was so reported after an outbreak of cholera in his station), you and your aunt very naturally took him for me, and, starting with that impression, every-thing he said corroborated it. Moreover, we have a strong resemblance to each other; only, as he thinks, he is so very much a finer fellow than I am. Now may I tell you my side of the story? It will not tire you?"

"Oh, no; I am curious to hear it," said Olive, playing nervously with the border of her shawl.

"Well, when I let myself write that— that letter — for which I must ask your pardon presently—I hoped I should be able to set out in less than a week. I was, however, unavoidably delayed. This gave my cousin the start of me. Knowing at this season Morley's might be full, I telegraphed from Malta for room, and on arriving was greeted by your letter of refusal. I had no right to expect anything from you ; but had you not written, I might at least have tried my chance. I was unreasonably disappointed, and determined not to stay in London. Next day I met Hubert, who told me he had renewed his acquaintance with you, and was evidently a good deal smitten. Putting all this together, I jumped at the conclusion that you had made up your mind to accept the elder cousin, and therefore were considerate enough to warn the rejected candidate off the premises. Am I now to believe that your letter was intended for Hubert—not for me ?"

"It was certainly intended for the Dr. Barclay who is stout, and loves a good dinner, and is bored with poor patients," returned Olive, with a sweet, gay laugh.

L

"Not for me?" insisted Horace.

"No, not for you," gravely. "Had your cousin not appeared, I should not have written anything; I should have waited——" She stopped abruptly.

"You would have given me a chance? Will you give me a chance, Olive?" again taking her hand, which lay unresistingly in his.

"If you still wish for one," she said in a low tone, "yes; but one cannot fall in love to order!"

"If you are not absolutely averse to me, Olive, I think I can teach you, for, unreasonable or not, I love you well! With all your softness, you are a plucky, sensible little darling; you behaved beautifully, in spite of your terror, the other day, and I am half ashamed of the delight I felt in holding you, though I fear you were suffering all the time."

"Hush!" murmured Olive, blushing quickly.

"To think, too," continued Horace, "that I was absolutely running away from you—no! do let me hold your hand; it is such a little bit of a hand! — when I was, or my driver was, nearly the death of you! I can never believe you will send me adrift now."

"Have you no doubts about your own wisdom?" began Olive, when Aunt Tabitha entered with a cup of beef tea.

"I'm thinking that Olive will be wanting a little refreshment," she said; "and I hope that you have settled matters between yourselves, for I am that tired with the obstinacy of some folk," significantly, "that I'd fain know what we are going to do."

"I am entirely in Olive's hands," said Horace Barclay, looking into her eyes, "and will patiently await her decision."

"As soon as I am able to write you another little note with this poor right hand," said Olive, with a sweet, shy upward glance, "you shall know——"

"If it's to be, or not to be!" put in Aunt Tabitha; "and in promising so much, my bairn, you promise a good deal."

Three months later, Dr. H. C. Barclay was bidden to the marriage of Dr. H. C. Barclay, jun. He came out well on that occasion, and presented his cousin's bride with a bracelet of cat's-eyes, set in diamonds, in remembrance of their original acquaintance. He was busy and jolly at the wedding, and whispered to more than one of his married lady friends that he was "deuced near cutting out the bridegroom— give you my word!"

THE MELANCHOLY HUSSAR

THE MELANCHOLY HUSSAR

By THOMAS HARDY

CHAPTER I.

ERE stretch the downs, fresh and breezy and green, absolutely unchanged since those eventful days. A plough has never disturbed the turf, and the sod that was uppermost then is uppermost now. Here stood the camp; here are distinct traces of the banks thrown up for the horses of the cavalry, and spots where the midden-heaps lay are still to be observed. At night, when I walk across the lonely place, it is impossible to avoid hearing, amid the scourings of the wind over the grass-bents and thistles, the old trumpet and bugle calls, and the rattle of the halters; to help seeing rows of spectral tents and the *impedimenta* of the soldiery. From within the canvases come guttural syllables of foreign tongues, and broken songs of the fatherland; for they were mainly regiments of the King's German Legion that slept round the tent-poles hereabout at that time.

It was nearly ninety years ago. The British uniform of the period, with its immense epaulettes, queer cocked-hat, breeches, gaiters, ponderous cartridge - box, buckled shoes, and what not, would look strange and barbarous now. Ideas have changed;

invention has followed invention. Soldiers were monumental objects then; a divinity still hedged kings here and there; and war was considered a glorious thing.

Secluded old manor houses and hamlets lie in the ravines and hollows among these hills, where a stranger had hardly ever been seen, till the King chose to take the baths yearly at the seaside watering-place a few miles to the south; as a consequence of which battalions descended in a cloud upon the open country around. Is it necessary to add that the echoes of many episodic tales, dating from that picturesque time, still linger about here, in more or less fragmentary form, to be caught by the attentive ear? Some of them I have repeated; most of them I have forgotten;

one I have never repeated, and assuredly can never forget.

Phyllis told me the story with her own lips. She was then an old lady of seventy-five, and her auditor a lad of sixteen. She enjoined silence as to her share in the incident till she should be " dead, buried, and forgotten." Her life was prolonged twelve years after the day of her narration, and she has now been dead nearly twenty. The oblivion which in her humility and modesty she courted for herself, has only partially fallen upon her, with the unfortunate result of inflicting an injustice upon her memory; since such fragments of her story as got abroad at the time, and have been kept alive ever since, are precisely those which are most unfavourable to her character

It all began with the arrival of the York Hussars, one of the foreign regiments above alluded to. Before that day, scarcely a soul had been seen near her father's house for weeks. When a noise like the brushing skirt of a visitor was heard on the door-step, it proved to be a scudding leaf; when a carriage seemed to be nearing the door, it was her father grinding his sickle on the stone in the garden, for his favourite re-laxation of trimming the box-tree borders to the plots. A sound like luggage thrown down from the coach was a gun far away at sea; and what looked like a tall man by the gate at dusk, was a yew-bush cut into a quaint and attenuated shape. There is no such solitude in country places now as there was in those old days.

Yet all the while King George and his Court were at Weymouth, not more than five miles off.

The daughter's seclusion was great, but beyond the seclusion of the girl lay the seclusion of the father. If her social condition was twilight, his was darkness. Yet he enjoyed his darkness, while her twilight oppressed her. Dr. Grove had been a professional man whose taste for lonely meditation over metaphysical questions had diminished his practice till it no longer paid him to keep it going; after which he had relinquished it and hired at a nominal rent the small, dilapidated manor house of this obscure inland nook, to make a sufficiency of an income which in a town would have been inadequate for their maintenance.

He stayed in his garden the greater part of the day, growing more and more irritable with the lapse of time, and the increasing perception that he had wasted his life in the pursuit of illusions. He saw his friends less and less frequently. Phyllis became so shy that if she met a stranger anywhere in her short rambles she felt ashamed at his gaze, walked awkwardly, and blushed to her shoulders.

Yet Phyllis was discovered even here by an admirer, and her hand most unexpectedly asked in marriage.

The King, as aforesaid, was at Weymouth, where he had taken up his abode at Gloucester Lodge; and his presence in the town naturally brought many county people thither. Among these idlers—many

of whom professed to have connections and
interests with the Court—was one Humphrey
Gould, a bachelor; a personage neither young
nor old; neither good-looking nor positively
plain. Too steady-going to be "a buck"
(as fast and unmarried men were then
called), he was an approximately fashion-
able man of a mild type. This bachelor
of thirty found his way to the village on
the down; beheld Phyllis; made her father's
acquaintance in order to make hers; and
by some means or other she sufficiently
inflamed his heart to lead him in that
direction almost daily; till he became engaged to marry her.

As he was of an old local family, some
of whose members were held in respect
in the county, Phyllis, in bringing him

to her feet, had accomplished what was considered a brilliant move for one in her constrained position. How she had done it was not quite known to Phyllis herself. In those days unequal marriages were regarded rather as violating the laws of nature than as a mere infringement of convention, the more modern view; and hence when Phyllis, of the Weymouth *bourgeoisie*, was chosen by such a gentlemanly fellow, it was as if she were going to be taken to heaven, though perhaps the uninformed would have seen no great difference in the respective positions of the pair, the said Gould being as poor as a crow.

This pecuniary condition was his excuse—probably a true one—for postponing their union; and as the winter drew nearer, and the King departed for the season, Mr. Humphrey Gould set out for Bath, promising to return to Phyllis in a few weeks. The winter arrived, the date of his promise passed, yet Gould postponed his coming, on the ground that he could not very easily leave his father in the city of their sojourn, the elder having no other relative near him. Phyllis, though lonely in the extreme, was content. The man who had asked her in marriage was a desirable husband for her in many ways; her father highly approved of his suit; but this neglect of her was awkward, if not painful, for Phyllis. Love him in the true sense of the word, she assured me she never did, but she had a genuine regard for him; admired a certain methodical and dogged way in which he sometimes took his pleasure; valued his knowledge of what the Court was doing, had done, or was about to do; and she was not without a feeling of pride that he had chosen her when he might have exercised a more ambitious choice.

But he did not come; and the spring developed. His letters were regular though formal; and it is not to be wondered that the uncertainty of her position, linked with the fact that there was not much passion in her thoughts of Humphrey, bred an indescribable dreariness in the heart of Phyllis Grove. The spring was soon summer, and the summer brought the King; but still no Humphrey Gould. All this while the engagement by letter was maintained intact.

At this point of time a golden radiance·

flashed in upon the lives of people here, and charged all youthful thought with emotional interest. This radiance was the York Hussars.

CHAPTER II.

THE present generation has probably but a very dim notion of the celebrated York Hussars of ninety years ago. They were one of the regiments of the King's German Legion, and (though they somewhat degenerated later on) their brilliant uniform, their splendid horses, and, above all, their foreign air and mustachios (rare appendages then), drew crowds of admirers of both sexes wherever they went. These, with other regiments, had come to encamp on the downs and pastures, because of the presence of the King in the neighbouring town.

Phyllis, though not precisely a girl of the village, was as interested as any of them in this military investment. Her father's home stood somewhat apart, and on the highest point of ground to which the lane ascended, so that it was almost level with the top of the church tower in the lower part of the parish. Immediately from the outside of the garden wall the grass spread away to a great distance, and it was crossed by a path which came close to the wall. Ever since her childhood it had been Phyllis's pleasure to clamber up this fence and sit on the top—a feat not so difficult as it may seem, the walls in this district being built of rubble, without mortar, so that there were plenty of crevices for small toes.

She was sitting up here one day, list-lessly surveying the pasture without, when her attention was arrested by a solitary figure walking along the path. It was one of the renowned German Hussars, and he moved onward with his eyes on the ground, and with the manner of one who wished to escape company. His head would pro-bably have been bent like his eyes, but for his stiff neck-gear. On nearer view she perceived that his face was marked with deep sadness. Without observing her, he advanced by the footpath till it brought him almost immediately under the wall.

Phyllis was much surprised to see a

fine, tall soldier in such a mood as this. Her theory of the military, and of the York Hussars in particular (derived entirely from hearsay, for she had never known a soldier in her life), was that their hearts were as gay as their accoutrements.

At this moment the Hussar lifted his eyes and noticed her on her perch, the white muslin neckerchief which covered her shoulders and neck where left bare by her low gown, and her white raiment in general, showing conspicuously in the bright sunlight of this summer day. He blushed a little at the suddenness of the encounter, and, without halting a moment from his pace, passed on.

All that day the foreigner's face haunted Phyllis; its aspect was so striking, so handsome, and his eyes were so blue, and sad, and abstracted. It was perhaps only natural that on some following day, at the same hour, she should look over that wall again, and wait till he had passed a second time. On this occasion he was reading a letter, and at the sight of her his manner was that of one who had half expected or hoped to discover her. He almost stopped, smiled, and made a courteous salute. The end of the meeting was that they exchanged a few words. She asked him what he was reading, and he readily informed her that he was reperusing letters from his mother in Germany; he did not get them often, he said, and was forced to read the old ones a great many times. This was all that passed at the present interview, but others of the same kind followed.

Phyllis used to say that his English, though not good, was quite intelligible to her, so that their acquaintance was never hindered by difficulties of speech. Whenever the subject became too delicate, subtle, or tender for such words of English as were at his command, the eyes no doubt helped out the tongue, and — though this was later on—the lips helped out the eyes. In short, this acquaintance, unguardedly made, and rash enough on their part, developed and ripened. Like Desdemona, she pitied him, and learnt his history.

His name was Matthäus Tina, and Saarbruck his native town, where his mother was still living. His age was twenty-two, and he had already risen to the grade of corporal, though he had not long been in the army. Phyllis used to assert that no such refined or well-educated young man could have been found in the ranks of the purely English regiments; some of these foreign soldiers having rather the graceful manner and presence of our native officers than of our rank and file.

She by degrees learnt from her foreign friend a circumstance about himself and his comrades, which Phyllis would least have expected of the York Hussars. So far from being as gay as its uniform, the regiment was pervaded by a dreadful melancholy, a chronic home-sickness, which depressed many of the men to such an extent that they could hardly attend to their drill. The worst sufferers were the younger soldiers who had not been over here long. They hated England and English life ; they took no interest whatever in King George and his island kingdom, and they only wished to be out of it and never to see it any more. Their bodies were here, but their hearts and minds were always far away in their dear fatherland, of which—brave men and stoical as they were in many ways—they would speak with tears in their eyes. One of the worst of the sufferers from this home woe, as he called it in his own tongue, was Matthäus Tina, whose dreamy, musing nature felt the gloom of exile still more intensely from the fact that he had left a lonely mother at home with nobody to cheer her.

Though Phyllis, touched by all this, and interested in his history, did not disdain her soldier's acquaintance, she declined (according to her own account, at least) to permit the young man to overstep the line of mere friendship for a long while —as long, indeed, as she considered herself likely to become the possession of another; though it is probable that she had lost her heart to Matthäus before she was herself aware. The stone wall of necessity made anything like intimacy difficult; and he had never ventured to come, or to ask to come, inside the garden, so that all their conversation had been overtly conducted across this boundary.

CHAPTER III.

BUT news reached the village from a friend of Phyllis's father, concerning Mr. Humphrey Gould, her remarkably cool and patient betrothed. This gentleman had been heard to say in Bath that he considered his overtures to Miss Phyllis Grove to have reached only the stage of a half-understanding; and in view of his enforced absence on his father's account, who was too great an invalid now to attend to his affairs, he thought it best that there should be no definite promise as yet on either side. He was not sure, indeed, that he might not cast his eyes elsewhere.

This account — though only a piece of hearsay, and as such entitled to no absolute credit—tallied so well with the infrequency of his letters and their lack of warmth, that Phyllis did not doubt its truth for one moment; and from that hour she felt herself free to bestow her heart as she should choose.   Not so her father; he declared the whole story to be a fabrication.   He had known Mr. Gould's family from his boyhood; and if there was one proverb which expressed the matrimonial aspect of that family well, it was "Love me little, love me long." Humphrey was an honourable man, who would not think of treating his engagement so lightly.

"Do you wait in patience," he said; "all will be right enough in time."

From these words Phyllis at first imagined that her father was in correspondence with Mr. Gould; and her heart sank within her; for, in spite of her original intentions, she had been relieved to hear that her engagement had come to nothing. But she presently learned that her father had heard no more of Humphrey Gould than she herself had done; while he would not write and address her *fiancé* directly on the subject, lest it should be deemed an imputation on that bachelor's honour.

"You want an excuse for encouraging one or other of those foreign fellows to flatter you with his unmeaning attentions," her father exclaimed, his mood having of late been a very unkind one towards her. "I see more than I say. Don't you ever set foot outside that garden-fence without my permission. If you want to see the camp, I'll take you myself some Sunday afternoon."

Phyllis had not the smallest intention of disobeying him as to her actions, but she assumed herself to be independent with respect to her feelings. She no longer checked her fancy for the Hussar, though she was far from regarding him as her lover in the serious sense in which an Englishman might have been regarded as such. The young foreign soldier was almost an ideal being to her, with none of the appurtenances of an ordinary house-dweller; one who had descended she knew not

N

whence, and would disappear she knew not, whither; the subject of a fascinating dream —no more.

They met continually now — mostly at dusk—during the brief interval between the going down of the sun and the minute at which the last trumpet-call summoned him to his tent. Perhaps her manner had become less restrained latterly; at any rate, that of the Hussar was so; he had grown more tender every day, and at parting after these hurried interviews, she reached down her hand from the top of the wall that he might press it. One evening he held it so long that she exclaimed: "The wall is white, and somebody in the field may see your shape against it."

He lingered so long that night that it

was with the greatest difficulty that he could run across the intervening stretch of ground and enter the camp in time. On the next occasion of his awaiting her she did not appear in her usual place at the usual hour. His disappointment was unspeakably keen; he remained staring blankly at the wall, like a man in a trance. The trumpets and tattoo sounded, and still he did not go.

She had been delayed purely by an accident. When she arrived she was anxious because of the lateness of the hour, having heard the sounds denoting the closing of the camp as well as he. She implored him to leave immediately.

"No," he said, gloomily. "I shall not go in yet—the moment you come—I have thought of your coming all day."

"But you may be disgraced at being after time?"

"I don't mind that. I should have disappeared from the world some time ago if it had not been for two persons—my beloved, here; and my mother in Saarbruck. I hate the army. I care more for a minute of your company than for all the promotion in the world."

Thus he stayed and talked to her, and told her interesting details of his native place, and incidents of his childhood, till she was in a simmer of distress at his recklessness in remaining. It was only because she insisted on bidding him good-night and leaving the wall that he returned to his quarters.

The next time that she saw him he was

without the stripes that had adorned his
sleeve. He had been broken to the level of
private for his lateness that night; and as
Phyllis considered herself to be the cause
of his disgrace, her sorrow was great. But
the position was now reversed; it was his
turn to cheer her.

"Don't grieve, *meine Liebliche!*" he said.
"I have got a remedy for whatever comes.
First, even supposing I regain my stripes,
would your father allow you to marry
a non-commissioned officer in the York
Hussars?"

She flushed. This practical step had not
been in her mind in relation to such an
unrealistic person as he was; and a moment's
reflection was enough for it.

"My father would not—certainly would

not," she answered, unflinchingly. "It cannot be thought of! My dear friend, please do forget me; I fear I am ruining you and your prospects!"

"Not at all!" said he. "You are giving this country of yours just sufficient interest to me to make me care to keep alive in it. If my dear land were here also, and my old parent, with you, I could be happy as I am, and would do my best as a soldier. But it is not so. And now listen. This is my plan. That you go with me to my own country, and be my wife there, and live there with my mother and me. I am not a Hanoverian, as you know, though I entered the army as such; my country is Bavaria by right, and is at peace with France, and if I were once in it I should be free."

"But how get there?" she asked.

Phyllis had been rather amazed than shocked at his proposition. Her position in her father's house was growing irksome and painful in the extreme; his parental affection seemed to be quite dried up. She was not a native of the village, like all the joyous girls around her; and in some way Matthäus Tina had infected her with his own passionate longing for his country, and mother, and home.

"But how?" she repeated, finding that he did not answer. "Will you buy your discharge?"

"Ah, no," he said; "that's impossible in these times. No; I came here against my will, why should I not escape? Now is the time, as we shall soon be leaving here, and I might see you no more. This is my scheme. I will ask you to meet me on the highway two miles off, on some calm night next week that may be appointed. There will be nothing unbecoming in it, or to cause you shame; you will not fly alone with me, for I will bring with me my devoted young friend, Christoph, who has lately joined the regiment, and who has agreed to assist in this enterprise. We shall have come from Weymouth Harbour, where we shall have examined the boats, and found one suited to our purpose. Christoph has already a chart of the Channel, and we will then go to Weymouth, and at midnight cut the boat from her moorings, and row away round the point out of sight; and by the next morning we are on the coast of

France, near Cherbourg. The rest is easy, for I have saved money for the land journey, and can get a change of clothes. I will write to my mother, who will meet us on the way."

He added details in reply to her inquiries, which left no doubt in Phyllis's mind of the feasibility of the undertaking. But its magnitude almost appalled her; and it is questionable if she would ever have gone further in the wild adventure if, on entering the house that night, her father had not accosted her in the most significant terms.

"How about the York Hussars?" he said

"They are still at the camp; but they are soon going away, I believe."

"It is useless for you to attempt to cloak your actions in that way. You have been meeting one of those fellows; you have been walking with him — foreign barbarians, not much better than the French themselves! I have made up my mind— don't speak a word till I have done, please! — I have made up my mind that you shall stay here no longer while they are on the spot. You shall go to your aunt's."

It was useless for her to protest that she had never taken a walk with any soldier or man under the sun except himself. Her protestations were feeble, too, for though he was not literally correct in his assertion, he was virtually only half in error.

The house of her father's sister was a prison to Phyllis. She had quite recently undergone experience of its gloom; and when her father went on to direct her to pack what would be necessary for her to take, her heart died within her. In after years she never attempted to excuse her conduct during this week of agitation; but the result of her self-communing was that she decided to join in the scheme of her lover and his friend, and fly to the country which he had coloured with such lovely hues in her imagination. She always said that the one feature in his proposal which overcame her hesitation, was the obvious purity and straightforwardness of his intentions. He showed himself to be so virtuous and kind; he treated her with a respect to which she had never before been accustomed; and she was braced to the obvious risks of the voyage by her confidence in him.

IT was on a soft, dark evening of the following week that they engaged in the adventure. Tina was to meet her at a point in the highway at which the lane to the village branched off. Christoph was to go ahead of them to the harbour, where the boat lay, row it round the Nothe — or Look-out, as it was called in those days — and pick them up on the other side of the promontory, which they were to reach by crossing the harbour bridge on foot, and climbing over the Look-out hill.

As soon as her father had ascended to his room she left the house, and, bundle in hand, proceeded at a trot along the lane. At such an hour not a soul was afoot anywhere in the village, and she reached the junction of the lane with the highway unobserved. Here she took up her position in the obscurity formed by the angle of a fence, whence she could discern every one who approached along the turnpike road, without being herself seen.

She had not remained thus waiting for her lover longer than a minute—though from the tension of her nerves the lapse of even that short time was trying—when, instead of the expected footsteps, the stage-coach could be heard descending the hill. She knew that Tina would not show himself till the road was clear, and waited impatiently for the coach to pass. Nearing the corner where she was, it slackened speed, and, instead of going by as usual, drew up within a few yards of her. A passenger alighted, and she heard his voice. It was Humphrey Gould's.

He had brought a friend with him, and luggage. The luggage was deposited on the grass, and the coach went on its route to Weymouth.

"I wonder where that young man is with the horse and trap?" said her former admirer to his companion. "I hope we shan't have to wait here long. I told him ten o'clock precisely."

"Have you got her present safe?"

"Phyllis's ? Oh, yes ; it is in this trunk. I hope it will please her."

"Of course it will. What woman would not be pleased with such a handsome peace-offering ? "

"Well, she deserves it. I've treated her rather badly. But she has been in my mind these last two days much more than I should care to confess to everybody. Ah, well; I'll say no more about that. It cannot be that she is so bad as they make out. I am quite sure that a girl of her good sense would know better than to get entangled with any of those Hanoverian soldiers. I won't believe it of her, and there's an end on't."

More words in the same strain were casually dropped as the two men waited;

words which revealed to her, as by a sudden illumination, the enormity of her conduct. The conversation was at length cut off by the arrival of the man with the vehicle. The luggage was placed in it, and they mounted and were driven on in the direction from which she had just come.

Phyllis was so conscience-stricken that she was at first inclined to follow them; but a moment's reflection led her to feel that it would only be bare justice to Matthäus, to wait till he arrived, and explain candidly that she had changed her mind—difficult as the struggle would be when she stood face to face with him. She bitterly reproached herself for having believed reports which represented Humphrey Gould as false to his engagement, when from what she

o

now heard from his own lips she gathered
that he had been living full of trust in
her; but she knew well enough who had
won her love. Without him her life seemed
a dreary prospect; yet the more she looked
at his proposal, the more she feared to accept
it—so wild as it was, so vague, so venture-
some. She had promised Humphrey Gould,
and it was only his assumed faithlessness
which had led her to treat that promise
as naught. His solicitude in bringing her
these gifts touched her; her promise must
be kept, and esteem must take the place
of love. She would preserve her self-respect.
She would stay at home, and marry him,
and suffer.

Phyllis had thus braced herself to an
exceptional fortitude when, a few minutes

later, the outline of Matthäus Tina appeared behind a field-gate, over which he lightly leapt as she stepped forward. There was no evading it, he pressed her to his breast.

"It is the first and last time!" she wildly thought, as she stood encircled by his arms.

How Phyllis got through the terrible ordeal of that night she could never clearly recollect. She always attributed her success in carrying out her resolve to her lover's honour, for as soon as she declared to him in feeble words that she had changed her mind, and felt that she could not, dare not, fly with him, he forbore to urge her, grieved as he was at her decision. Unscrupulous pressure on his part, seeing how romantically she had become attached to him, would no doubt have turned the balance in his favour. But he did nothing to tempt her unduly or unfairly.

On her side, fearing for his safety, she begged him to remain. This, he declared, could not be. " I cannot break faith with my friend," said he. Had he stood alone, he would have abandoned his plan. But Christoph, with the boat, and compass, and chart, was waiting on the shore ; the tide would soon turn ; his mother had been warned of his coming ; go he must.

Many precious minutes were lost while he tarried, unable to tear himself away. Phyllis held to her resolve, though it cost her many a bitter pang. At last they parted, and he went down the hill. Before his footsteps had quite died away, she felt a desire to behold at least his outline once more, and running noiselessly after him, regained view of his diminishing figure. For one moment she was sufficiently excited to be on the point of rushing forward and linking her fate with his. But she could not. The courage which at the critical instant failed Cleopatra of Egypt could scarcely be expected of Phyllis Grove.

A dark shape, similar to his own, joined him in the highway. It was Christoph, his friend. She could see no more; they had hastened on in the direction of the harbour. With a feeling akin to despair she turned and slowly pursued her way homeward.

Tattoo sounded in the camp; but there was no camp for her now. It was as dead as the camp of the Assyrians after the passage of the Destroying Angel.

She noiselessly entered the house, seeing nobody, and went to bed. Grief, which kept her awake at first, ultimately wrapped her in a heavy sleep. The next morning her father met her at the foot of the stairs.

"Mr. Gould is come!" he said, triumphantly.

Humphrey was staying at the inn, and had already called to inquire for her. He had brought her a present of a very handsome looking-glass in a frame of *repoussé* silver-work, which her father held in his hand. He had promised to call again in the course of an hour, to ask Phyllis to walk with him.

Pretty mirrors were rarer in country

houses at that day than they are now, and
the one before her won Phyllis's admiration.
She looked into it, saw how heavy her eyes
were, and endeavoured to brighten them.
She was in that wretched state of mind which
leads a woman to move mechanically onward
in what she conceives to be her allotted
path. Mr. Humphrey had, in his undemon-
strative way, been adhering all along to the
old understanding; it was for her to do
the same, and to say not a word of her
own lapse. She put on her bonnet and
tippet, and when he arrived at the hour
named she was at the door awaiting him.

CHAPTER V.

PHYLLIS thanked him for his beautiful gift; but the talking was soon entirely on Humphrey's side as they walked along. He told her of the latest movements of the world of fashion—a subject which she would willingly have discussed to the exclusion of anything more personal—and his measured language helped to still her disquieted heart and brain. Had not her own sadness been what it was, she must have observed his embarrassment. At last he abruptly changed the subject.

"I am glad you are pleased with my little present," he said. "The truth is that I bought it to propitiate 'ee, and to get you to help me out of a mighty difficulty."

It was inconceivable to Phyllis that this independent bachelor—whom she admired in some respects—could have a difficulty.

"Phyllis, I'll tell you my secret at once; for I have a monstrous secret to confide before I can ask your counsel. The case is, then, that I am married; yes, I have privately married a dear young belle; and if you knew her, and I hope you will, you would say everything in her praise. But she is not quite the one that my father would have chose for me—you know the paternal idea as well as I—and I have kept

it secret. There will be a terrible row, no
doubt; but I think that with your help
I may get over it. If you would only do
me this good turn—when I have told my
father, I mean—say that you never could
have married me, you know, or something
of that sort — 'pon my life, it will help
to smooth the way mightily. I am so
anxious to win him round to my point
of view, and not to cause any estrange-
ment."

What Phyllis replied she scarcely knew,
or how she counselled him as to his un-
expected situation. Yet the relief that his
announcement brought her was perceptible.
To have confided her trouble in return
was what her aching heart longed to do;
and had Humphrey been a woman, she

would instantly have poured out her tale. But to him she feared to confess; and there was a real reason for silence, till a sufficient time had elapsed to allow her lover and his comrade to get out of harm's way.

As soon as she reached home again she sought a solitary place, and spent the time in half regretting that she had not gone away, and in dreaming over the meetings with Matthäus Tina from their beginning to their end. In his own country, amongst his own countrywomen, he would possibly soon forget her, even to her very name.

Her listlessness was such that she did not go out of the house for several days. There came a morning which broke in fog and mist, behind which the dawn could be discerned in greenish gray, and the outlines of the tents, and the rows of horses at the ropes. The smoke from the canteen fires drooped heavily.

The spot at the bottom of the garden where she had been accustomed to climb the wall to meet Matthäus, was the only inch of English ground in which she took any interest; and in spite of the disagreeable haze prevailing, she walked out there till she reached the well-known corner. Every blade of grass was weighted with little liquid globes, and slugs and snails had crept out upon the plots. She could hear the usual faint noises from the camp, and in the other direction the trot of farmers on the road to Weymouth, for it was market day. She observed that her frequent visits to this corner had quite trodden down the grass in the angle of the wall, and left marks of garden - soil on the stepping - stones by which she had mounted to look over the top. Seldom having gone there till dusk, she had not considered that her traces might be visible by day. Perhaps it was these which had revealed her trysts to her father.

While she paused in melancholy regard, she fancied that the customary sounds from the tents were changing their character. Indifferent as Phyllis was to camp doings now, she mounted by the steps to the old place. What she beheld at first awed and perplexed her; then she stood rigid, her fingers hooked to the wall, her eyes staring out of her head, and her face as if hardened to stone.

On the open green stretching before her, all the regiments in the camp were drawn up in a square, in the midst of which two empty coffins lay on the ground. The unwonted sounds which she had noticed came from an advancing procession. It consisted of the band of the York Hussars playing a dead march; next two soldiers of that regiment, guarded on each side, and accompanied by a clergyman. Behind came a crowd of rustics who had been attracted by the event. The melancholy procession entered the square, and halted beside the coffins, where the two condemned men were blindfolded, and each placed kneeling on his coffin; a few minutes' pause was now given, while they prayed.

A firing-party of twelve stood ready with levelled carbines. The commanding officer, who had his sword drawn, waved it through some cuts of the sword exercise till he reached the downward stroke, whereat the firing-party discharged their volley. The two victims fell, one upon his face across his coffin, the other backwards.

As the volley resounded there arose a shriek from the wall of Dr. Grove's garden, and some one fell down inside; but nobody among the spectators without noticed it at the time. The two executed hussars were Matthäus Tina and his friend Christoph. The soldiers on guard placed the bodies in the coffins almost instantly; but the colonel of the regiment, an Englishman, rode up and exclaimed in a stern voice:

" Turn them out—as an example to the men ! "

The coffins were lifted endwise, and the dead Germans flung out upon their faces on the grass. Then all the regiments were marched past the spot, and when the survey was over the corpses were again coffined, and borne away.

Meanwhile Dr. Grove, attracted by the noise of the volley, had rushed out into his garden, where he saw his wretched daughter lying motionless against the wall. She was taken indoors, but it was long before she recovered consciousness, and for weeks they despaired of her reason.

It transpired that the luckless deserters

from the York Hussars had cut the boat from her moorings in Weymouth Harbour, according to their plan, and, with two other comrades who were smarting under ill-treatment from their colonel, had sailed in safety across the Channel; but mistaking their bearings, they steered into Jersey, thinking that island the French coast. Here they were perceived to be deserters, and delivered up to the authorities. Matthäus and Christoph interceded for the other two at the court-martial, saying that it was entirely by the former's representations that these were induced to go. Their sentence was accordingly commuted to flogging, the death punishment being reserved for their leaders.

The visitor to Weymouth, who may

P

care to ramble to the neighbouring village
under the hills, and examine the register
of burials, will there find two entries in
these words :

"Matth : Tina (Corpl.) in His Majesty's
Regmt. of York Hussars, and Shot for
Desertion, was Buried June 30th, 1801,
aged 22 years. Born in the town of Sars-
bruk, Germany.

"Christoph Bless belonging to His Majesty's Regmt. of York Hussars, who was
Shot for Desertion, was Buried June 30th,
1801, aged 22 years. Born at Lothaargen,
Alsatia."

Their graves were dug at the back of
the little church, near the wall. There
is no memorial to mark the spot, but Phyllis
pointed it out to me. While she lived she

used to keep their mounds neat; but now they are overgrown with nettles, and sunk nearly flat. The older villagers, however, who know of the episode from their parents, still recollect the place where the soldiers lie. Phyllis lies near.

THE END

LONDON: SPENCER BLACKETT, ST. BRIDE STREET, E.C.